WDM PRESENTS: SHORT FICTION FROM 2020

DEB LOGAN

DEBBIE MUMFORD

WDM
Publishing

INTRODUCTION

2020. What a year! Despite the pandemic (or maybe because of it), WDM Publishing had a fulfilling year. We're excited to share the short fiction we published during those most unusual months.

Our authors tended to combat the isolation and bleakness of real life events by writing lighter tales. Deb Logan wrote early reader and middle grade stories, while Debbie Mumford looked forward into mankind's adventures in deep space.

This volume opens with a sweet romance, moves into the realm of young childhood, before exploring the far reaches of space through the eyes of both adult explorers and a preteen girl living on a space station. Finally, we end the volume with two very different contemporary fantasies.

2020 was a year like no other, but it still produced some great fiction. We hope you enjoy the year's stories.

OPENING HER EYES

1

*E*mily Jane Williams chewed the nail of her right index finger and stared at her computer monitor. The glowing words mocked her with their blatant invitation to experience life beyond her small Rocky Mountain town.

<Crusader says: Join me in Shanghai. I'll make it my mission to show you a good time.>

The chat room friend she'd been fantasizing about for the past six months wanted to meet her... in a place as far from her normal life as she could imagine. Adventure. Desire. Danger. Those words belonged in novels, not in Emily's staid, placid life. A shiver tingled down her spine and she squirmed in her well-worn secretarial chair.

She ran trembling hands through her long brown hair and licked lips gone suddenly dry. This called for a witty remark, something that downplayed the rapid staccato of her heart. Unfortunately, her unsteady fingers moved with a life of their own.

<Sleeping Beauty says: Why now? Why Shanghai?>

Emily had lived her entire twenty-eight years in one place: Aspen Springs, Colorado. Her big adventure had been to spend her four years of college on the Front Range, at the University of Colorado's Boulder campus. She'd never been out of her home state, let alone out of the country. The thought of going to Shanghai, even to meet a man as fascinating as Crusader, filled her with terror.

<Crusader says: Why not now? A knight must meet his Lady, the one he's destined to adore.>

A frisson of delight spread through her core. Crusader always knew the right button to push. Knights and ladies, castles and dragons, these were images that made Emily's soul sing. Sometimes she felt like she'd known this mysterious man forever.

Mysterious. That was the operative word. She frowned and forced herself to think, to remember that she knew nothing about this man. Unwillingness to leave the United States aside, she had no business making plans to meet an Internet stranger. For all she knew, he could be a psychotic killer.

Or the love she'd waited for her whole life...

<Crusader says: What do you say? Are you up for an adventure?>

Her spine stiffened at the implied challenge.

<Sleeping Beauty says: Shanghai? No way! If I agree to meet you, it'll have to be here, on my home turf.>

That would put an end to his nonsense. Any man adventurous enough to choose Shanghai as a rendezvous would be totally uninterested in her little world.

<Crusader says: Name the time and the place. I'll be there.>

Emily's jaw dropped. She gasped like one of the brown trout she'd pulled from the clear, mountain stream last Saturday. He'd come *here*? He couldn't come here! What would a man like Crusader want in Aspen Springs?

The answer welled up like spring water, filling her with crystal coolness. Only one thing: her.

_E_very Monday morning since they'd returned to Aspen Springs from their respective colleges, Emily and Daria Roberts had met for breakfast at Katy's Kountry Kitchen. The ritual kept them close. Today, Emily wondered if that was a good thing.

"You told him where you live?" Daria stared at Emily, eyes wide, fingers drumming. "Have you lost your mind?"

Sunlight streamed across the freshly scrubbed oak of their favorite table as Emily considered her friend's words. Maybe she _had_ stepped over the threshold of sanity. The diner's familiar scents of sizzling bacon, frying eggs, and black coffee clashed dangerously with the thought of an unknown man traveling from who knew where to meet her.

"It's not like I gave him my address. I just told him about Aspen Springs." Daria's expression told Emily that wasn't much of an improvement. "For heaven's sake, I'm not an idiot. I'll be careful."

"Not an idiot? Well, you're sure doing a great imitation of one." Daria huffed, clasped her hands to still their drumming, and attempted a smile. "At least tell me when and where you're meeting him. That way Tim and I can wander by, make sure you're safe."

Emily's rebellious side wanted to clam up, but her instinct for self-preservation won. "Sure. He's meeting me at O'Connor's at 7:00 Saturday night." She looked down at the sturdy ceramic coffee mug clasped in white-knuckled fingers. "But you don't have to worry. He won't be there."

Daria reached across the table, placed her hand on Emily's arm and squeezed. "Maybe not, but we will."

Emily heaved a sigh of relief and glanced gratefully into Daria's dark blue eyes. They were such opposites. Blue-eyed, blonde Daria, with her luscious curves and Germanic forthrightness, and dark-eyed, dark-haired Emily, slim and athletic, with a quiet, though stubborn personality. Maybe they'd become friends in preschool because of those differences. Emily didn't much care; Daria's steadfast support grounded her world.

With a wry grin, Emily changed the subject. "What's Chris up to these days?" Daria's little brother had been the bane of their existence growing up, but she hadn't seen the little monster since he earned his place as commanding officer of a SEAL team based out of California. Hard to imagine the perennial pest in a position of leadership.

Daria grimaced. "His career choice scares the blazes out of Mom, but he's doing fine. We never know where he is, of course, but he calls frequently, so we know he's okay."

"I can't imagine," Emily said, her voice thick with sarcasm. "Somebody actually gave him a gun. Heaven help us!"

Daria's grimace turned into a mischievous grin. "Right? He's a born trouble-maker. Remember that time he cut a notch out of your hair?"

Emily rolled her eyes. "As if I could forget! Mom had to cut my hair in a bob. I hated it."

"And his absolute obsession with that chocolate cake from

Larson's Bakery?" Daria asked, her eyes glazing with the memory. "You know, the one with double fudge frosting."

Emily nodded, her expression softening. "It's a wonder he wasn't as round as he was tall. He bought that cake nearly every weekend once he started earning money mowing lawns in summer and shoveling snow in winter."

"Good times," Daria said, grabbing Emily's hand and interlocking their fingers. "And good friends. We're so lucky, Em!"

3

_____

Daria pegged it, Emily thought. *My mind isn't just lost; it's fried.*

Saturday morning found her sitting in a beautician's chair having her hair styled and highlighted. She hadn't allowed anyone to touch her hair in years. But here she was, submitting her dignity and total lack of style to the hands of a teen-age girl with spiky purple hair.

"There you go, Ms. Williams." The girl smiled at Emily's reflection in the mirror. "You're now the hottest county planner in the state."

Emily's cheeks flamed a scorching red.

"Thanks," she said, scrutinizing her new do. The shoulder length brown hair swung freely, tips curling under in tidy conformity. Fresh, golden highlights hinted at days spent lazing in the sun.

"I feel like a new woman. You don't give advice on clothes, do you?"

The girl giggled, reminding Emily of the difference in their ages. "My style wouldn't suit you, but if you're serious, you should ask for Jean over at *Tres Chic*. She's my cousin, and she knows all the latest trends."

Emily thanked the girl, paid and walked out into the bright spring sunshine. The air was so clear she felt like she could see each individual needle on the pines covering the mountain slopes. And the scent! High country wildflowers bloomed in profusion in the meadows surrounding the town. What a glorious time to be alive.

Her heart sang, and then stuttered as thoughts of meeting Crusader clashed with her ebullient mood. She had just over eight hours before their appointed meeting, and she didn't even own a decent cocktail dress.

Ignoring the mountains' allure, she straightened her shoulders and headed to *Tres Chic*, hoping the spiky-haired teen-ager had given her good advice.

For the next couple of hours, Emily allowed Jean to supervise her wardrobe choices. The young hairdresser was right; Jean had superb taste.

Emily had been hoarding her salary for years, so money wasn't an issue, but she still felt her heart stutter when she noticed the price tags.

Quick to recognize sticker shock, Jean said, "Don't worry, we don't have to empty your closet and start over today." She led Emily to a dressing room, picking out a few classic pieces as she went. "We'll set you up with some basic coordinates. You can add to it a piece at a time."

With a sigh of relief, Emily allowed herself to be prodded down the path to a more stylish wardrobe.

4

――――――――

*S*aturday night found Emily seated at a table near O'Connor's dance floor. The establishment was an interesting mix of restaurant, bar, and dance club. Small enough to survive in a little mountain town, but big enough to give its patrons room to breathe on a Saturday night.

True to her word, Daria sat at the bar with her husband, Tim. Her fingers tapped a swizzle stick in rapid syncopation as she scrutinized her friend.

Emily sympathized with Daria's agitation – a combination of nerves about the coming rendezvous and shock over Emily's appearance. Emily hadn't looked this good since college, and even then she'd lacked the sense of style Jean had so carefully crafted.

So, here she sat, a beautifully groomed young woman resisting the urge to bite her newly manicured nails. Crusader had better show.

She heard a low whistle and turned to find Chris Peterson standing beside her chair. Daria's younger brother shared her Germanic solidity, but his eyes were a deep chocolate brown, his complexion was ruddier than his sister's, and his hair skimmed the border between blond and brown, seeming to shift from chestnut to golden. He had just arrived home from a tour of duty overseas and looked fit and tanned.

"Wow," he said, taking in every detail of her flirty red dress and freshly styled hair. "You're a knock-out, Emily."

She looked past him to the door, and then met his eyes. "Thanks, and welcome home, but... I'm meeting someone." Emily didn't want to be rude, but she didn't want him ruining her chances with Crusader, either.

"I know you are, and I must say, he's a lucky man." Chris pulled out the chair opposite her and deposited his lanky six-foot frame on it.

"Chris! Get up!" Irritation heated her cheeks. "I can't believe Daria told you about this, but I *am* expecting someone – and I don't want you butting in."

He smiled; a maddening, slow smile. The kind that had driven her nuts when they were kids. When Chris smiled like that, he was up to something. "Daria didn't tell me. *Crusader* did."

Her pulse skipped a beat. She focused on Chris, everything else blurring into the background. She hadn't told Daria Crusader's screen name.

"Where did you hear that name?" she asked, aware of every heartbeat, every breath that flowed through her lungs.

Chris reached across the table and took her hand. "Wake up, Sleeping Beauty. It's time to see the world as it really is." He stroked her fingers with his thumb. "*I'm* Crusader."

She snatched her hand away, jumped to her feet and turned to leave. Before she'd gone two steps, Chris blocked her path.

"Great idea," he said. "Let's dance."

He used Emily's own momentum to maneuver her onto the dance floor. With his strong arms encircling her, she had to force herself to think. Her body wanted to melt into his embrace.

She pushed back and peered up into his handsome face. "What are you up to, Chris? Why the big mystery? If you wanted a date, why didn't you just ask?"

He threw back his head and laughed until other patrons stared. When the fit passed, he dropped his head close to hers and said, "Emily, you're amazing, but you're totally clueless. I've been asking you out since high school. You've just never taken me seriously."

He tightened his embrace and rubbed his chin across her newly golden hair. "I had some leave coming; I wanted to see you. Crusader seemed like a good tactic." He shrugged and added, "Daria gave me your screen name."

For once in her life, Emily was speechless. She delighted in the thrill of her old nemesis's warm embrace and marveled that she'd been looking right through him her whole life. Daria's little brother had grown into quite a man.

"What would you have done if I'd agreed to meet you in Shanghai?"

"I'd have hopped a military transport," he said, his blue eyes sparkling, "but I knew you wouldn't." He guided her effortlessly across the dance floor. "I wanted Crusader to shake you up. Make you look at yourself and see what I see – a fascinating, sexy woman."

Emily blushed and lowered her gaze.

"But mostly, I wanted—"

She never found out what he'd wanted, because Daria chose that moment to tap Chris' shoulder and throw her arms around her brother's neck. "Chris! Why didn't you tell me you were coming to O'Connor's tonight?"

Emily didn't wait to hear his answer. She grabbed the opportunity to retreat, despite his best efforts to catch and hold her hand. Unsure what to think about the evening's unexpected turn of events, she grabbed her purse and practically ran home.

5

After spending Sunday holed up in her home like a prospector protecting his claim, Emily awoke Monday morning with a fresh resolve. No more hiding in the house for this woman. She glared at her reflection in the bathroom mirror as she scrubbed her teeth.

"I've got no reason to be embarrassed," she stated, pointing her toothbrush at her foamy-mouthed reflection. She spit, rinsed, and continued her pep talk, "I didn't hide my identity and try to pull a fast one on anybody. Chris is the one who should be ashamed. We're too old to be playing stupid pranks."

She dressed quickly in her jogging outfit and pulled her hair into a pony tail while reminding herself again that Chris' only objective had been to embarrass her. He'd felt like a bit of mischief and had reverted to his childhood target of choice... his big sister's best friend, Emily.

Stepping onto the tiny front porch of her rustic-looking two-bedroom log cabin, she paused to lock the door and stow her key in the specially designed pouch in the laces of her left running shoe. She was still kneeling when she felt his presence. Straightening, she found herself looking up at Chris.

And damn, did he look good. Navy blue sweat pants, white tee pulled taut across a muscular chest and an unzipped hooded navy sweatshirt – the man fairly oozed testosterone. She raised her eyes to meet his gaze and concentrated on producing an icy glare. Not an easy task when her blood sizzled like liquid fire.

"I'm leaving for my morning jog, Chris." Her words dripped sleet. She congratulated herself on her poise in the face of raging attraction. "I don't have time for you."

"Fine," he said. "I'm not stopping you."

She turned away from him and began to run in easy rhythmic strides. He loped along beside her. She ignored him, reached the corner and turned toward the mountain trail that ran behind her subdivision. Chris turned with her.

"What do you think you're doing?" she asked, continuing to edge her words with ice.

"Jogging," he said. "I run five to ten miles every day. This is as good a trail as any."

"Choose another one," she snapped. "I don't want your company."

"It's a public trail, and I didn't start this conversation," he pointed out. "If you don't want to talk, don't."

Emily opened her mouth to reply, but changed her mind and clamped her lips together. Fine. If he wanted to play games, she was his match any day.

She stopped beside the bench at the base of the trail and ran through her usual set of stretches. He ran through his own routine beside her. She tried to keep her attention on the scenery, but her eyes betrayed her, stealing sideways peeks at the healthy male form striking poses beside her. Okay, so he wasn't actually posing, but those rippling muscle groups made a fine display. Daria's little brother made exceptional eye-candy.

Stop it, she told herself. *You're not interested in anything about this man.*

A self-satisfied smirk tugged at her lips as she ran lightly down the dirt trail. *Man? Yeah, right. This is Chris, remember? The pest who spied on you and Daria and followed you around like a stray dog; the insect who cut a notch out of your hair in fourth grade; the idiot who interrupted your first real make-out session with David Lang. This isn't a man; this is Chris... the closest thing you'll ever have to a brother. Thinking of him as eye-candy is, well, it's incestuous! Gross. Get a grip.*

Her resolve strengthened, Emily picked up the pace despite the path's increasing slope. She ran this trail daily. Her body knew every twist, every stray root and stone. Her breathing regulated and her brain kicked into its automatic pilot phase, leaving her free to contemplate the beauty of the mountain's early morning haze.

Chris loped along beside her when the path widened, dropped back where it narrowed. She felt his eyes on her derriere and stomped on the soaring elation that her butt was firm and perfectly packed into her spandex tights. He was vermin, not a man she wanted to entice.

She reached the high meadow where she always slowed to a walk, and Chris flew past her. Resolutely, she kept her eyes on the spring wildflowers filling the meadow with riotous color. This walking portion of her morning routine gave her heart and other muscles a bit of a rest before she started the knee-pounding descent back into her ordinary world.

Emily loved this mountain. In point of fact, she loved the entire Rocky Mountain Range, though she'd only seen sections of its glory – the parts within her home state. She'd climbed all of Colorado's 'fourteeners' with her dad. They'd started with Long's Peak at the south end of Rocky Mountain National Park when she'd been fourteen. Dad thought it an auspicious start to her climbing career. She still found climbing fourteen-thousand foot peaks an exhilarating experience, but it wasn't one she could have on a regular basis. However, she jogged this trail daily, and hiked other nearby trails as often as she could. The season was just beginning, and she looked forward to revisiting all her favorite sites this spring and summer.

She picked up her pace and headed for home, congratulating herself on Chris' conspicuous absence. She'd done it. She'd outlasted the irritating man. The path turned around a thick stand of budding aspens and she caught sight of his navy blue sweats. Her pace faltered. Maybe she should walk the rest of the way down, avoid contact.

Hell, no. She wouldn't give him the satisfaction. Besides, if she changed her pace that much, it would throw her off schedule for the rest of the morning. She straightened her shoulders and resumed her normal rhythm.

Chris seemed to be waiting for her to catch up. He glanced back with a grin and then resumed his own long-legged stride.

Emily was left with an excellent view of his perfectly toned butt and legs. She groaned and thanked heaven that the mornings remained too cool for shorts; sweats showed her more than enough. She tried to distract herself with the scenery, but thick trees and undergrowth edged this part of the path. Her eyes kept moving forward and latching hungrily on Chris' very appealing anatomy.

6

*C*hris jogged down the trail toward Emily's cabin. He'd thoroughly enjoyed the view on his way up. If anything, Emily was more attractive now than she'd been in high school. She'd ripened into a sexy, well-toned woman. According to Daria, Em still enjoyed hiking, backpacking, and fly fishing. All the things he was looking forward to doing when he retired from the SEALS and returned to civilian life.

He'd set his sights on Emily while they were still kids, and despite all the places his military career had taken him, he'd never found anyone to break that single-minded focus. Emily Jane Williams was the woman for him.

Now all he had to do was convince her that while he'd always be her best friend's brother, he was also an adult man with a mind of his own... and that he was singularly devoted to her.

Saturday night's mission hadn't gone exactly as planned, but he was a SEAL. He knew how to improvise in the field. He'd been disappointed by the delay caused by her determination not to leave her cabin yesterday, but he'd known she'd have to emerge this morning. She had a job, and she had a routine. And he was well aware of her habits, having casually turned his conversations with Daria to Emily on a fairly regular basis.

Daria was an excellent source of intel. Not that she'd known she was acting as such. She'd been genuinely surprised to see Chris dancing with Emily at O'Connor's on Saturday night. But she was clued-in now, and almost giddy with the prospect of claiming Emily as an honest-to-goodness sister. He'd have to remind is truthful-to-the-core, straightforward sister not to over-play her hand.

After all, Chris had to win Emily on his own merits, not just because she adored his family.

Chris frowned as he dodged a tree root. Em had been frosty this morning. She'd probably convinced herself that he was pulling a prank on her, making her the butt of a joke. A slow smile spread across his face. Hopefully his own well-muscled butt was gaining her attention at the moment. He'd certainly enjoyed watching hers earlier.

Yanking his thoughts away from her shapely posterior, he considered how to go about convincing her that his intentions were true, that he was honestly attracted to her... and had been since he was old enough to understand such things.

He reached the bench where they'd done their warm up stretches and turned to watch her jog her last few steps. He'd always thought the cliché that "women didn't sweat, they glowed" was malarkey, but, wow! Emily proved the sentiment. Even sweaty from a trail run, she was a knock-out.

He dropped into his cool down routine in order to stop himself from staring. She was skittish enough without him drooling on her running shoes.

Well, he'd done what he could for the morning. Now the ball was in Daria's court. He just hoped his sister's innate honesty wouldn't cause her to fumble the play.

7

_E_mily joined Daria at their favorite table at Katy's, relieved that Chris hadn't followed her to breakfast. The man had dogged her steps all the way back to her front door. Fortunately, he'd been gone when she emerged again after showering and changing into her work clothes – a slim black pencil skirt, white silk blouse, and a lightweight charcoal gray sweater.

He'd rattled her enough that she was almost late meeting Daria.

"So," Daria said, a smile curving her lips, "how was your run this morning?"

Emily's eyes narrowed and she was about to accuse her best friend of colluding with the enemy when the waitress arrived with a steaming pot of coffee. Just breathing in that scent relaxed Emily's jaw and dissipated a bit of the morning's irritation.

"How are you ladies this morning?" the young woman asked as she poured coffee into white ceramic mugs. "Do you want the usual, or would you like to see the menu?"

"My usual, please," Emily said, picking up her coffee and blowing across the steaming surface.

"Got it. Two eggs over easy, a rasher of bacon, and whole wheat toast. No butter."

She turned expectantly to Daria.

"I'm feeling adventurous today," she said. "Bring me French toast and a side of bacon."

"Okey-dokey. I'll get that right up."

As she walked away, Emily turned a suspicious gaze on Daria. "What do you know about Chris turning up for my morning run?"

Daria avoided her gaze and stirred a packet of sugar into her coffee. Finally she looked up, expression as innocent as a puppy's, and said, "Chris joined you for your run? How nice."

"Nice?" The word exploded from Emily's lips. She leaned across the table and glared at her so-called best friend. "You think it's *nice* that he's trying to make a fool out of me?"

"What?" Daria yelped. "Is that what you think? Em, you've got it all wrong!"

"Did you know he was coming home to meet me? All that time I was telling you about the guy I'd met in that chat room... did you know it was Chris?"

"Of course not! Emily, I wouldn't do that to you, and no matter what you think, Chris is *not* pulling a prank."

Emily closed her eyes, took a deep breath, and forced herself to relax. When she felt a bit more grounded, she opened her eyes and studied Daria. Her lifelong friend was pale, her blue eyes wide and frightened. She extended her hand toward Emily, paused, and pulled it back. Her fingers shook.

"Emily," she whispered. "Please... say something."

The waitress arrived with their breakfast. She slid their plates in front of them with practiced ease, smiled, topped off their coffee, and bustled away.

Scents of bacon, fried eggs, and maple syrup wafted enticingly around the table, but neither woman touched her food.

They sat as if turned to stone, staring into each other's eyes; one suspiciously, the other beseechingly.

After what felt like hours, Emily lowered her eyes. "We'd better eat," she said. "We don't want to be late to work."

Daria shook her head. "I'm not hungry. Call me later if you want to talk."

Emily grabbed Daria's hand before she could leave the table. "Don't go," she said quietly. "I'm sorry. I shouldn't have accused you of being in on this... whatever *this* is."

Daria twisted her hand in Emily's and locked their fingers together. "Chris might be my brother," she said, "but you've always been closer than a sister, Em. I'd never intentionally hurt you."

"I know," Emily said, squeezing her friend's fingers. They released each other's hands. "Shall we start over? Forget Chris exists?"

Daria laughed. "Easier said than done. Who knew he'd still be a pest at this age?"

The knots in Emily's stomach eased and she realized she actually was hungry. Suddenly the plate before her smelled fabulous and looked even better. She attacked her breakfast with gusto, pushing Chris to the back of her mind.

When her plate had been reduced to a smear of egg yolk and grease, she wiped her mouth and fingers on her napkin, glanced at her watch, and smiled at Daria. "Looks like we'll make it to work on time after all."

Daria smiled weakly, lowered her gaze, and played with her fork.

"What?" asked Emily, her suspicions aroused.

"Well, it's just..." Daria licked her lips, then met Emily's gaze and plunged in. "I don't want to upset you, but I promised."

Emily sighed. "Okay. I'm braced. What does Chris want you to do?"

"You're the best, Em," Daria said with a genuine smile, "and it's not just Chris, it's the whole family. We'd like you to come over tonight for a 'welcome home' barbeque. Chris will be there, of course, but so will Mom and Dad and Tim and I."

"Of course I'll come," Emily said after only a moment's hesitation. "Your house or your parents'?"

"Mom and Dad's." Relief glowed on Daria's face. "About 7:00, and Tim and I won't let Chris corner you. I promise."

Emily laughed. "That's okay. I'll be safe with your mom and dad there. Even Chris wouldn't dare get out of line with his mom watching!"

Daria grinned. "That's the truth. See you tonight."

---

8

*E*mily stopped at Larson's Bakery on her way home from work and bought Chris' favorite dessert: a chocolate layer cake with double fudge frosting. She told herself it was for the whole family, after all the Petersons were all chocolate fanatics, but she knew she was lying to herself. Chris had been crazy about that cake since he was a kid. She was buying it for him.

She stopped by her cabin just long enough to kick off her low heels, scramble out of her work clothes and pull on a comfortable forest green T-shirt and her favorite denim jeans. After lacing on her hiking boots, she grabbed the cake box and headed down the street and over a block to the Peterson's home.

Emily and Daria had grown up practically next door to each other, their respective homes being across the street and down one house from each other, but when Emily's parents retired last year, they'd moved down to Golden where the weather was a bit milder and the snow didn't pile up quite as high as it did in the mountains surrounding Aspen Springs. Just walking through the neighborhood stirred up childhood memories, but the Peterson home... well, that solid, two-story Craftsman house with its gable roof, spacious front porch, and creamy yellow board and batten siding was like a second home to her.

She followed the cement walk to the front porch and rang the doorbell. When the door swung open, Chris stood there looking even more delicious than he had that morning. He could've been a young god in black jeans and deep russet T-shirt.

"Hey, Em," he said, his baritone voice setting off harmonics that reverberated through her nervous system. "Glad you could come."

"Of course," she said, thrusting the cake box into his hands as she struggled not to ogle his stunningly muscled chest and arms. "I wouldn't dream of missing a barbeque with your folks."

A flicker of irritation crossed his features, but he smiled and waved her inside. "Come on in. Everyone's in the back yard."

Emily stepped past him, noting the spicy scent of his cologne – something citrusy with a hint of sandalwood – and continued down the hall, through the family room and out the sliding glass door to the patio.

Chris, right behind her, called, "Look who's here! And she came bearing gifts!"

Papa Peterson looked up from a grill laden with burgers and brats and waved a set of barbeque tongs at her. "Hey, Emily. Glad you're here. Wouldn't be a family party without you."

Mama Peterson bustled over from the picnic table, strategically located on the shadiest part of the flagstone patio, and pulled Emily into a motherly hug. "What have we here?" she asked, lifting the lid on the cake box in her son's hands.

Chris peered inside as well and whooped when he saw the cake. "Booyah! It's chocolate cake." He grinned at Emily and winked. "I knew I liked you!"

"Good thing he's holding that box," Daria said, coming to

stand beside her friend, "or he'd be twirling you in a circle just now. You know how nuts he is about chocolate cake."

Emily laughed. "And not just any chocolate cake. It's from Larson's and that's double fudge frosting."

Chris moaned. "Can we forget dinner and move straight to dessert?" he asked his mom, his eyes pleading.

She laughed and swatted his arm. "Go put that cake on the table. And keep your fingers out of the frosting." She shook her head and followed him across the patio. "You'd think you were still ten instead of a grown man... and a military officer, at that."

Dinner at the Peterson's was delightful. Just like always. They gathered around the picnic table and ate Papa P's perfectly grilled burgers and brats, the meat so juicy the buns couldn't soak it all up. Emily's fingers were soon a sticky mess, but that didn't stop her from enjoying Mama P's homemade potato salad or Daria's contribution of fresh broccoli and bacon slaw. If Emily had been worried about being uncomfortable in Chris' presence, she shouldn't have. The family chattered and joked just as they always had.

After the meal was finished and the chocolate cake had been devoured, Daria and Emily cleared the table and put the leftovers in the fridge, while Tim and Chris cleaned the grill and gathered the trash. Mr. and Mrs. Peterson were relegated to lounge chairs in the backyard while the *youngsters* took care of what Chris termed *KP*.

When the chores were done, Chris approached Emily with an outstretched hand. "Would you walk with me, Em?"

Daria straightened, punched Tim in the ribs, and moved to join her best friend. But Emily smiled and shook her head. Instead, she accepted Chris' hand. "I'd like that."

She and Chris left the backyard by the gate and strolled along the side of the house to the front street. "What was that all about?" he asked.

Emily tucked her hand into the crook of his arm and gazed down the street. So many memories. Bicycle races. Sword fights with cardboard wrapping paper tubes. Sledding on the hill behind the Peterson home. And through good times and bad, her steadfast friend... Daria.

"Nothing. Just Daria being my friend."

"And I'm not?"

She laughed aloud. "No! You were the pesky the little brother." She stopped and looked up at him. "And for the last couple of days, I've been thinking of you as the enemy."

He quirked an eyebrow at her, but remained quiet.

"When Daria invited me to dinner tonight, she promised that she and Tim wouldn't let you corner me. She knew I was upset, but..."

He waited, the expression in his dark eyes intense. "But?" he encouraged.

She turned and walked forward, tugging gently on his arm. When they'd established an easy rhythm, she continued. "Dinner tonight reminded me who we all are. We're family, Chris, and whatever you're doing, you're not trying to hurt me. You're not my enemy. Never have been, never will be."

This time it was Chris who stopped. "I'm not your brother, either," he said, his voice quiet, but firm. "Never have been. Never wanted to be."

He took both of her hands in his and waited for her to meet his gaze. "I'm not teasing you, Emily. I outgrew the desire to tug your pigtails a long time ago. I love you and I'd like the chance to find out if you can love me, too."

Emily stared into the face of this man she'd known forever, and yet not known at all. A shiver of possibility ran down her spine, and she dropped her gaze.

"When Daria interrupted us Saturday night, I didn't get the chance to finish what I was saying, about why I used the

Crusader persona," he paused, his fingers tightening around hers. "Like I said, I wanted Crusader to shake you up. Make you look at yourself and see what I see – a fascinating, sexy woman. But mostly, I wanted to throw you off balance so you'd have to open your eyes and really *see* me." He reached up and stroked her cheek with a single finger. "Not Daria's kid brother; not the boy who teased you in school." He placed that finger beneath her chin and, very gently, lifted. "I wanted you to see *me...* the man who's been crazy about you for years."

She lifted her face and their eyes met. A spark ignited and fire raced through her body.

"Can you see me yet, Emily?"

She swallowed, throat suddenly parched. "Yes, Chris." Her voice sounded husky, somehow raw. "I see you."

He roared with delight, scooped her off her feet, and lifted her into the air.

Emily gazed down at this man who'd been willing to cross the world to be with her... and wondered how she'd missed the love shining in his eyes.

COPYRIGHT

CHATTERMASTER

*B*lake loved to talk. He rarely closed his mouth.

He chatted with his parents over protein shakes at breakfast. He gabbed to his friends on the way to the educational unit. He whispered answers to himself when his instructor called on someone else. He even chanted in a singsong rhythm during recess in the exercise pod.

Sometimes his happy chatter annoyed other people.

"Don't talk with food in your mouth, Blake," Mother said at dinner one night. She spoke distinctly because the ship's galley brimmed with colonists. Most family units ate at six bells.

"But..."

Father held up one finger, preventing his son's reply.

Blake deflated. He'd only wanted to point out his mouth was empty.

"It's dinner time, Blake," said Father. "Get some food in your mouth."

Obediently, Blake bit into the replicated chicken, chewed and swallowed before opening his mouth. Mother spoke first.

"Tomorrow is a big day for you, Blake," she said, pausing to sip recycled water. "Master Farmer Jaden has agreed to test you for a possible apprenticeship."

Blake's mouth gaped, but no words came out. Master Farmer Jaden grew all the food for the Starship *Generations*. Blake's parents worked alongside the great man in the hydroponics gardens.

"You should be honored," said Father. "The Master Farmer rarely tests applicants."

Early the next morning Blake marched into the hydroponics pod. The chamber hummed with activity. Rows upon rows of green plants towered above stainless steel troughs. Pumps whirred, circulating nutrient-rich liquid to nourish the plants that fed the ship's occupants. Farmers and apprentices made careful adjustments or harvested ripe fruit.

Blake waved to Mother and Father. They smiled and nodded toward the Master Farmer's office.

At Blake's approach, the office doors whooshed open to reveal the Master Farmer hunched over a computer console. Wispy white hair framed a wrinkled face. Antique glasses perched upon his nose. When he looked up, faded brown eyes measured Blake.

"Good. You're prompt," said the old man. He straightened and strode past Blake out the door. "Walk with me and tell me what you know of gardening, boy."

Blake raced to keep up with the man's long-legged stride. The invitation to talk thrilled him.

"Both my parents are farmers," he said, "so I know lots about plants. This garden is so efficient, it feeds the whole ship. Nothing is wasted."

Blake happily parroted information gained during visits to the garden. He explained how the plants grew in liquid without icky, old-fashioned dirt. Blake gabbled non-stop, barely pausing to breathe.

Master Farmer Jaden stopped outside a chamber on the far side of the hydroponics pod. He raised a hand to stem Blake's chatter. Silver-green silence bloomed.

Blake waited.

The Master Farmer remained still.

Blake fidgeted, but kept quiet.

After what felt like ages, Master Farmer Jaden spoke. "Well, boy, it is clear you have an active mind and can absorb what you are told. Certainly, you communicate well. Both are qualities I will require in my next apprentice."

"That's wonderful, sir," said Blake. "I'd love to be your apprentice. Father always says…"

He trailed off at the old man's raised eyebrow.

Silence ruled again.

Blake squirmed under Master Farmer Jaden's gaze, but kept his lips together.

Finally, the Master Farmer spoke. "I will watch your progress, boy. When you're twelve, if you've learned the value of silence, you'll be my next apprentice.

"Make no mistake; this will be a challenging position. Your parents were born on this ship and have lived their whole lives with hydroponics, but things are changing. My next apprentice will be required to learn the secrets of this chamber."

The old man waved a hand and the chamber doors whooshed open.

Warm moist air greeted Blake as he stepped onto a dark, cushiony surface. An unfamiliar odor teased his nose. He sniffed cautiously and then inhaled deeply.

Master Farmer Jaden nodded. "That smell is dirt. These plants are growing in it. You're standing on it, too."

Blake glanced down. His thin-soled shoes sank into a mushy brown substance.

"Dirt?"

"Yes, dirt." The old man observed Blake's confusion, smiled and laid a hand on his shoulder. "You see, boy, this ship will reach planetfall during the prime of your life. My next apprentice must learn the art of growing food in dirt. This small chamber has been preserved for generations to train the first planetside farmer.

"What do you think, Blake? Will you be up to the challenge?"

Blake squatted and touched the dirt. He pinched a bit, brought his fingers to his nose and savored the rich, distinctive aroma. Quiet warmth blossomed in his chest; he'd found his calling.

"Yes, sir!" he said. Blake grinned broadly—and closed his mouth.

COPYRIGHT

CHATTERMASTER
Copyright © 2020 by Debbie Mumford
Published by WDM Publishing
Cover and Layout copyright © 2020 by WDM Publishing
Cover design by WDM Publishing
Cover art copyright
© NatashaFedorova | Depositphotos.com

DEIRDRE'S DRAGON

*D*eirdre rubbed her eyes, and then stared open-mouthed at the dragon squished onto the window seat. He was shiny, golden, and too big to be believed.

The dragon oozed off the cushion onto the hardwood floor. He yawned and stretched, reminding Deirdre of a really big (make that gigantic!) cat.

She stood perfectly still, heart pounding so hard her fingers and toes felt like they might explode. She wondered if the dragon was hungry, but mostly she wondered what dragons ate.

"Caviar," the dragon rumbled, licking his lips. "You know, little black fish eggs, but I'll settle for peanut butter and jelly on rye."

"You, uhh, you talked! Where did you come from? Wait a minute. I didn't say that out loud." Words gushed from Deirdre's mouth. She was standing in the library of Gran's Scottish mansion talking to a dragon, and all she could do was ask stupid questions.

"Of course I talk," said the dragon, "and I hear your thoughts, too." He lifted his lip in what Deirdre hoped was a dragon smile. "As to where I came from, why, you called me."

"I did? I didn't mean to. I mean, I'm sure you're a very nice dragon and all ..." her words trailed off. She took a deep breath and tried again. "How did I call you?"

"You touched that silver medal, and on your twelfth birthday, too." A wisp of smoke escaped his nostrils.

Deirdre hoped he didn't belch up a flame. With all these books, she'd be toast in a heartbeat! Oh, yeah, the medal. She glanced at the ornament clutched in her sweaty palm. The bright disk boasted a tiny picture of a dragon in mid-flight.

"I am bound to the females of your bloodline," the dragon continued, "but you must be twelve before I'm allowed to show myself." He lowered his head and looked straight into her eyes. "Happy birthday, Deirdre."

"Thank you." Mom would be pleased. Even with her mind in a whirl, Deirdre remembered her manners. Mom. Aha! "Does my mother know about you?"

"Of course." He turned his jewel-bright eyes away from Deirdre and glanced around the room. "She's heard all your Gran's stories, just as you have."

"No!" Deirdre cried, stamping her foot. "That's not what I mean, and you know it." She decided to be more specific. "Does my mother think you're real? Has she ever talked to you?"

The dragon ambled to the hearth and curled up in front of the extinct fire. "No." He yawned and nestled his triangular head onto his front feet. Claws flashed, and then retracted, rescuing the hearthrug from certain destruction.

"Why not?"

"The enchantment skips a generation. You won't be ready to give me up when your daughter turns twelve." His eyes sparkled, laughter dancing in their depths. "But when your granddaughter comes of age, well, that will be another bowl of caviar."

"Well ... what if I don't have a daughter? Or a granddaughter?"

His head jerked up, his eyes round as saucers. "No granddaughter? But you have to have a granddaughter!"

"No, I don't," Deirdre said, her heart skipped a beat. Arguing with a dragon might be dangerous, but this was important. "Mom says I can be anything I want." She planted her fists squarely on her hips and stared up into the dragon's glittering eyes. "Dad says so, too. I'm going to be an astronaut and discover new planets."

The dragon stared at her. His huge eyes whirled, and the spiky tip of his golden tail beat a rapid rhythm on the hearthrug. "Maybe you could have a daughter before you go exploring?"

She relaxed a little and considered his suggestion. "Maybe, but I might be too busy training. You might have to wait until I get back from my new planet."

He looked so disappointed. She wanted to ease the sting. "Maybe I'll name my first planet after you. Say, what is your name?"

He stood proudly on all four feet, wings furled tightly against his back and made a noise that sounded like chewing up rocks and gargling the slurry.

"Oh." She cleared her throat — it hurt just listening to that name – and said, "well, maybe I'd better just take you along when I go exploring." She paused, thought about that terrible noise, and asked, "I don't suppose you have a nickname?"

He grinned his toothy grin and said, "You may call me Roddy."

Voices in the hall interrupted them. Deirdre turned from the dragon to stare at the closed door. A moment later, it burst open and Dad stepped into the room.

"Hi, Dad," she said, stuffing the medal into the back pocket of her jeans. She glanced over her shoulder at Roddy.

The majestic beast was gone. In his place lay Gran's favorite toy — the dragon she'd told all her stories about.

CHAPTER 2

*L*ate that night, Deirdre snuggled under the covers of the huge bed in Gran's guest room. The old mansion whispered and creaked around her. Another night she might have been frightened, but not tonight.

Tonight Roddy lay stretched across the length of the bedroom floor. His huge bulk protected her from the unaccustomed night sounds.

"What if Mom comes in?" she whispered.

"She'll see a toy on the floor," he replied. "Go to sleep, Deirdre, you're safe with me."

She closed her eyes and thought about home. What was she going to do with a dragon in Denver?

"Have the time of your life," came the nearly silent answer. "We'll have wonderful adventures. Just wait and see."

COPYRIGHT

THE FOX AND THE FLEAS

*R*ory Fox sat beside his den on the grassy hillside. He scratched his furry red ears. A moment later he nipped at his back leg. Then he nibbled his shoulder.

Mother Fox looked up from grooming her long, bushy tail. "What's wrong, Rory?" she asked. "Why are you nipping and scratching?"

"I have fleas, Mother." He looked at her and blinked back tears. "They're biting me all over. I can't catch them with my teeth. What can I do?"

Mother Fox stood and flicked her ears. "Come with me, my son. It's time you learned how a fox deals with fleas."

So Rory followed his mother to the edge of Farmer McNabb's field. Once there, Mother Fox sat down and curled her tail around her toes. Rory tried to copy her, but the biting fleas made it hard to sit still.

"Now, Rory," she said, "do you see Mrs. Sheep out there in the meadow?"

Rory used his keen eyes to peer across the field. "Yes, Mother. She has her twin lambs with her."

Mother Fox nodded. "You must go and ask Mrs. Sheep for a bit of her wool. When you have it, meet me at the pond by those trees." She pointed her long nose at a thicket across the meadow. "Be polite, my son."

"Yes, ma'am," said Rory, and he trotted over to Mrs. Sheep.

As he approached the family, Rory said, "Good day, Mrs. Sheep." He sat down in the sun-warmed grass and tried not to squirm as the fleas bit his rump.

Mrs. Sheep stepped between Rory and her twins. "Wha-a-at can I do-o-o for yo-o-ou, little fox?" she asked.

"My mother told me to ask if you could spare a little wool," Rory answered, politely bowing his head.

"Wha-a-at do yo-o-ou want with wo-o-ol?" asked Mrs. Sheep.

"I'm being bitten by fleas," he admitted. "Mother is going to teach me how a fox deals with fleas."

"Ah-h-h," said Mrs. Sheep.

"Ah-h-h," echoed her lambs.

"There's a patch of my wo-o-ol on that stump by the thicket," Mrs. Sheep said. "Yo-o-ou are welcome to use it."

"Thank you, Mrs. Sheep," Rory said, remembering his manners.

Rory retrieved the scrap of wool and bounded off to find his mother. The fleas were biting his front legs now. He was very tired of being itchy.

He found Mother Fox sitting serenely beside the pond. She nodded her head when she saw the scrap of wool in Rory's mouth.

"Well done, my son," she said. "Now listen carefully. If you follow my instructions, the fleas will soon be gone."

Rory cocked his ears forward to catch every word. He wanted to do this right. He wanted the fleas to go away.

"You must hold the wool by the very edge, so almost none is in your mouth."

Rory laid the scrap on the ground and carefully picked it up by the smallest corner.

Mother Fox nodded. "Now, walk over to the pond and dip the tip of your tail in the water."

Rory obeyed. He felt the fleas run from his tail and move toward his rump.

"Now," said his mother, "move slowly and steadily backwards into the water."

Rory began to move. As each piece of his body went under the water, he felt the fleas run up to dry skin.

"That's right," said Mother Fox. "Keep going back until only your nose is above the water."

Rory hesitated. He could swim, but he didn't like getting his face wet.

"Trust me, Rory," said Mother Fox. "When only your nose is left above water, let the wool float away."

Rory took a deep breath and followed his mother's advice. As his head sank below the water's surface, he felt the fleas run across his nose and onto the wool. When the last flea jumped from the tip of his nose, he let go of the wool and swam straight to the shore.

Mother Fox sat in the cool grass with her tail wrapped tightly around her paws. She smiled a foxy smile as Rory shook the water from his coat and raced around the meadow. At last he flopped down beside her, happy that the fleas were gone.

"Well done, my son," she said. "Now you know how a fox deals with fleas."

COPYRIGHT

MOM'S HELPER

*B*enjamin looked up when his Irish Setter stopped digging; he watched the dog turn his slender snout toward the house. The big dog always heard Mom before Benjamin did. Benjamin listened really hard, but he didn't hear anything.

He wished he had ears like Rusty's.

He stretched out grimy fingers and stroked the long, silky

hair on Rusty's ear, then felt his own naked one. How could Rusty hear so much better when his ears were clogged with hair? Benjamin puzzled over this problem until he heard his mom's voice.

"Benjamin! Benjamin David, where are you?"

"Here, Mom." The sturdy little boy scrambled to his feet and ran around the corner of the house.

"What were you doing around there?" Mom's voice was tired. She was always tired these days. Tired and sad.

"Nuffin'." He scuffed the dirt with the toe of his red sneaker. "Helpin' Rusty."

The big red dog bounded up and danced on the cement at Mom's feet. She smiled at his antics and her shoulders dropped a fraction of an inch. "What did Rusty need help with?"

Benjamin heard the shift in Mom's tone and grinned up at her. "We're playin' with dirt. It's soft and squishy, and Rusty likes it a lot!"

Mom sighed and shook her head. "You're going to need a good scrubbing before dinner. Oh well, never mind that now. You and Rusty have fun, but stay where I can see you from the window."

"Okay, Mom." He turned to run across the sparse grass, Rusty trailing at his heels.

Benjamin didn't like this new backyard. There wasn't anything to do in it. Not like his old yard. That one had a swing set, a real pool, and a trampoline. Benjamin liked the trampoline best. He and his dad had lots of fun jumping on it.

Dad.

He didn't want to think about Dad. He wanted to play with Rusty.

Benjamin looked around. Where did Rusty go?

He moved down the fence line until he could see the side yard, but still be seen from the kitchen window.

There he was!

Rusty had returned to the hole he was digging in the cool, brown earth.

Benjamin hesitated. He wanted to go help Rusty dig, but he wanted to obey his mom, too.

The hot sun beating down on his blond head made the decision for him. There wasn't any shade in the part of the yard the window could see. All the shade was over there with Rusty and the hole.

Besides, he was Mom's Helper. He needed to take care of Rusty.

Benjamin helped Mom as much as he could. She was so sad since Dad ...

No. He wasn't going to think about that.

Mom needed him to keep an eye on Rusty.

His decision made, Benjamin ran across the yard to the growing mound of dirt next to the fence. Rusty looked up as he arrived and wagged his tail happily.

Benjamin settled himself on the ground and began arranging the soft, cool earth in neat little piles. Some he squished together in his hands, making lopsided balls. Some he pushed into hills and valleys and drew roads with his fingers.

He wished he had one of his trucks to drive on the roads, but he didn't want to get up and go inside. If he did, Mom would probably make him wash for dinner.

Road construction absorbed his attention so completely that he didn't notice when Rusty stopped digging and started wriggling.

Not until it was too late.

He heard a happy bark and looked up to find Rusty staring at him from the other side of the fence.

"Rusty! What are you doing out there?" Benjamin watched in horror as Rusty pranced toward the street.

"Rusty! Come back here!"

The big dog stopped, looked back at Benjamin and wagged his tail. Benjamin saw him wink, and knew Rusty wasn't coming back.

He should go get Mom. Mom would know what to do.

But Mom was so sad ... if Rusty ran away, she would be even more unhappy.

Benjamin looked from the dog to the house and then at the hole. He could do it. He could get through that hole and bring Rusty home.

Mom wouldn't know Rusty tried to run away. Mom wouldn't have something new to be sad about.

Benjamin was Mom's Helper. He could do this!

2

Benjamin laid down on his belly and squirmed across the cool dirt. When his head reached the fence he pushed it so close to the ground his left ear filled with grit ... but his head went under!

He kept squirming.

Once, he raised his shoulder a little too high and felt the fence scratch his skin, but it didn't hurt much. He pressed his shoulder closer to the earth and kept wriggling.

Rusty danced back to the fence, cheering him on with happy little yips.

Finally, he was through the hole. He stood up, brushed some of the dirt off his jeans and T-shirt and looked at his dog.

"That was very bad, Rusty," he scolded. "You get right back in our yard."

But Rusty had other ideas.

The big red dog dropped to a crouch and then bounded up to lick Benjamin in the face. Before Benjamin could recover, Rusty took off down the sidewalk.

Benjamin wiped his face on his shirt, looked once more at his home, and then ran after the happy dog.

Catching Rusty was an adventure.

Benjamin had never been out of his yard without an adult before. He felt very grown-up as he ran down the street after the red dog.

When he came to the first corner, Benjamin stopped. Rusty paused on the other side, watching to see what he would do.

Benjamin remembered what he'd learned about crossing streets. He looked first one way and then the other.

He didn't see any cars at all.

Carefully, he stepped into the street. Still no cars.

He dashed across, hoping to catch Rusty's collar, but the long-legged animal loped away before he got to the other side.

This game of run-and-wait lasted a long time, until they came to a busy street.

Benjamin struggled to keep up, to keep the dog in sight. He groaned as Rusty pranced into a knot of people just as the traffic light changed.

Before Benjamin could reach them, they'd crossed the street. Cars flowed across his path again.

Rusty sat on the far corner, his tail beating a lively rhythm on the sidewalk.

Benjamin looked around. He knew this place. This was the corner where Mom always stopped and waited for the red hand to turn to a white person before she jogged across the street, pushing Benjamin in the oversized stroller.

He looked at the traffic light. He saw a red hand. He waited.

Soon the traffic stopped and the light changed to the white man.

Benjamin stepped off the curb and, keeping his eyes on Rusty, ran across the street.

The cars moving past at his side scared him. His knees felt weak and wobbly, but he kept moving toward his dog.

Rusty seemed to understand Benjamin's fear. He sat very still, waiting for Benjamin to catch up.

When Benjamin stepped onto the sidewalk, he threw himself at the big red dog and hugged him tightly. Reassuring warmth flowed from the dog to the boy.

He did it!

He caught Rusty.

He helped Mom.

Now, he just had to take Rusty home.

3

Benjamin studied the street. He knew where he was, but he didn't know how to get home.

Rusty knew, but Benjamin couldn't trust Rusty to go straight home. He grabbed Rusty's collar and moved away from the busy corner.

He spied a wooden bench beside a store window and led Rusty to it. His knees still wobbled slightly as he climbed onto the bench.

"We have to go home, Rusty," he said, staring firmly into the dog's liquid brown eyes. "Mom's getting dinner ready."

Rusty rested his chin on Benjamin's lap. His eyes looked mournful.

"It's okay. You don't have to be sad. You didn't mean to run away." Benjamin stroked the dog's silky head.

He needed to think.

He couldn't follow Rusty home. Rusty might not go straight home.

He wasn't sure he could find the way back by himself. He needed help.

Dad always said if he got lost in the forest, he should hug a tree 'til Dad found him. But there weren't any trees here, and Dad ...

No. He wasn't going to think about Dad.

Mom said he should never go anywhere with a stranger, so he couldn't ask a grown-up.

Wait a minute! There was one grown-up he could ask.

Mom always said, "Policemen are our friends."

That was the answer. Benjamin needed to find a policeman.

He stood up and walked back to the corner, still holding Rusty's collar. The Irish Setter, tired of the game of chase, seemed content to stay close to Benjamin's side.

Benjamin looked down the street the way he'd come. He didn't see any policemen.

He looked the other direction. No one that way either.

He turned around and looked at the store window next to the bench. There were yellow curtains in the window, and lots of white letters on the glass.

Benjamin recognized the letters, but he didn't know what B- A- K- E- R- Y- spelled.

He thought about his problem for a minute, and decided that if he didn't go anywhere with her, it would be okay to ask a stranger to call the police for him.

He marched up to the store and right in the open door.

"Here, now," said a loud voice, "you can't bring that dog in here! Shoo ... outside with you." A huge woman dressed all in white rolled toward him. She shook a flour-covered finger at him.

Benjamin froze; he held Rusty's collar with both hands. His wide blue eyes filled with tears. He was tired of helping Mom.

He wanted to go home.

The woman came closer and knelt in front of Benjamin. She must have seen the tears, because she didn't sound angry anymore.

"What's the matter, little fellow?" she asked, her voice much softer now. "Are you and your dog lost?"

Benjamin nodded. "Rusty and me need a policeman, please."

Mom would be proud; Benjamin remembered his manners.

The woman smiled. "That's a very sensible request, young man." She took Benjamin's grubby little hand and led him to a table near the front door.

"I guess you and Rusty better sit here while you wait." She pointed her finger at Rusty. "You, sit!"

Rusty sat, then laid down at Benjamin's feet.

The woman looked surprised, and pleased.

"I'll be right back," she said as she bustled behind a counter filled with breads, cakes and cookies.

Feeling safer now, Benjamin noticed how sweet the air smelled. The sight and smell of food reminded him that he hadn't eaten yet.

He was really tired.

His legs twitched from running. His stomach growled and twisted, and his eyelids kept trying to close.

Helping Mom was hard work.

He stretched one foot out to touch Rusty, and laid his head and arms on the table.

4

*W*hen Chloe walked into the bakery, she thought her heart would burst with relief. There he was, her baby, safe and sound. She drank in the sight of her grimy little boy asleep at the café table with his big red dog stretched at his feet.

She turned to the police officer who accompanied her. "Yes, that's him. That's my son, Benjamin."

"I knew the minute the call came in that it had to be your boy." The officer smiled. "I'm still amazed he got this far. Two miles is a long way for a four-year-old to travel."

Chloe nodded. "Rusty must've been on his way to the dog park. I'm just glad they stopped here."

She turned and walked to the counter. "Thank you so much for giving him a place to wait, and for calling the police," she said to the bakery owner. "If anything had happened to him," her voice caught, and she paused a moment before continuing. "My husband died a few months ago. When I lost my house, too, I thought I'd lost everything."

She turned to look at her sleeping child. "I was wrong. My

world is sturdy and healthy, and very tired at the moment." She turned back and gave the woman a tearful smile.

"My pleasure, ma'am, and I must say, he's a good little fellow." She gave Chloe an answering grin. "Even if he did bring a dog into my bakery."

"Yes," said Chloe, "Benjamin's a good boy. His dad used to call him 'Mom's Helper.'"

The next day Benjamin helped Mom put a big rock in the hole where Rusty had escaped.

"If you see Rusty digging near the fence again," Mom said, shading her eyes with one hand, "what should you do?"

"I'll tell you and we'll find another big rock," Benjamin said with a grin.

"Perfect," said Mom. "That will be the best way for you to be my helper!"

Benjamin hugged Mom, then patted Rusty on the head and said, "C'mon, Rusty. Let's race to the house!"

COPYRIGHT

THE QUEEN'S CAPTIVE

1

$\mathscr{I}$ am a worm; the property of the Tse-Tsunxhanaga queen.

My people, the grotesque and rebellious humans of Earth and its feeble colonies, call the noble Tse-Tsunxhanaga hive *Bug-Eyes*. This detestable name came about because the insipid human vocal apparatus is unable to adequately pronounce the sublime clicks, hums, and sub-vocal stops of the elegant Tse-Tsunxhanaga language; also because the hive's superior exoskeleton bears a superficial resemblance to an ancient Earth insect: the cockroach.

My name is Zara. I am a human female. I was taken captive by the hive when my human colony was destroyed by the noble Tse-Tsunxhanaga. I was four earth-years old at the time. I have no idea of my current age, although I believe I have reached sexual maturity. I have not seen the open sky since the day I was taken. I am the property of Queen Tsetseg and am an object of study in her Royal Academy of Science. It is hoped that someday I will be capable of acting as an interpreter for the queen. However, my vulgar and inadequate vocal apparatus render this hope unlikely. While I understand the language of the hive, I am incapable of speaking it in any form fit for presentation to a personage as great and glorious as Queen Tsetseg.

I remain unworthy of her notice.

My body, soft and vulnerable as it is, requires frequent maintenance. Unsightly thread-like protuberances grow from my scalp, necessitating shaving. Since gaining maturity, these threads also appear in other places on my body. Removal is often painful. My keepers, the noble Tsagai, Tsila, and Tserig, despair of ever making me presentable, for in the process of cleansing, my delicate skin often turns unsightly shades of blue, green, or purple, and in some cases is torn, allowing my disgusting red bodily fluids to ooze forth. My keepers discovered early that if that red fluid should gush rather than ooze, my pitiful existence would be in danger of being extinguished. Worse yet, even when healed, the tears leave ugly blemishes upon my person.

I am covered with such scars.

Tsagai, Tsila, and Tserig, the keepers who have studied me since my arrival in the hive, often click their pincers in perplexity as to how such a fragile species could possibly have survived long enough to attain the knowledge required to build ships and journey to distant stars. They have often posited that I must be an aberration, a dysfunctional unit allowed to live for scientific purposes, perhaps to learn why my anomalies came into being.

Since I have almost no memory of my time among my own kind, I have been unable to enlighten my noble keepers as to the reason for my existence. However, as I am currently their only human specimen, my deformities are catalogued and I continue to be studied.

Recently, something went awry in one of Queen Tsetseg's campaigns to exterminate the vermin that are my species. I know this only because my keepers despair of my understanding and so feel free to discuss hive gossip in my presence.

Two of my keepers, Tsila and Tserig, had taken me to the hexagonal cell that served as my training center: a large, sterile white room with a glass enclosure on one wall where my keepers could seal themselves safely out of my reach, but still observe my every movement. I sat quietly on the antiseptically clean floor (there being no furniture in the room) perusing the electronic device my keepers allowed me to study. The device had been found in my domicile when my colony was destroyed, and the warriors who captured me brought it along, thinking it might provide clues to my care and feeding.

My keepers found it useless, but allowed me to play with it, thinking that the familiar unit from my home might soothe my early terrors. It was good that they did so, for the device was an educational tool and allowed me to learn to read my native tongue. It also held an encyclopedia of knowledge, which has allowed me to understand my people and their history.

My keepers are unable to read the human language, and I allow them to think the device contains no more than pretty pictures of the planet that gave rise to my species. What they do not know benefits me.

Tsagai, the most senior drone in the triad tasked with my study, entered my training center, his pincers clicking with excitement. "Have you heard?" he asked Tsila and Tserig, who were located in the glass enclosure, working at a long metallic counter piled high with the instruments and devices necessary to their research. The enclosure was not sealed against me; my keepers had long ago judged me incapable of harm. Tsila and Tserig were currently working on an enhancement collar, a device they hoped would allow me to speak intelligibly, but they put down their tools and turned their attention to Tsagai.

Tsila's anterior antennae waved in greeting. "Heard what?"

"The campaign to remove the vermin from CSG-159— the planet the vermin have named *Absaroka*— has failed. Our flagship was destroyed, and the fighters, left without support or retreat, were lost."

All movement in the room stilled as Tsila and Tserig processed this horrifying news.

I sat quietly on the hard, white floor, hardly daring to breathe. I desperately wanted to hear more. I couldn't imagine how humans, weak and fragile as I knew my species to be, could possibly have inflicted great harm on the Tse-Tsunxhanaga hive. Damage a few fighters, perhaps, but to destroy a flagship? Unthinkable! Perhaps my weakness was truly an aberration after all.

"Are you certain of your facts?" Tserig asked, his anterior and lateral antennae vibrating with agitation. "While I do not doubt your word, noble Tsagai, this report seems highly unlikely."

I agreed, but kept still, my eyes on the device in my lap, hardly daring to breathe lest they remember my presence and seal the enclosure, thereby ending my ability to listen.

All of Tsagai's antennae ruffled, then relaxed, proclaiming his authority. "My source is unimpeachable. Champion Tsagadai himself told me of the disaster."

Tsila and Tserig bowed their six-eyed heads and murmured in unison, "Praise be to the One from whom the Jelly flows!"

Silence reigned while my keepers processed this astounding information.

I had learned from my device that, while the hive's exoskeleton resembles a cockroach, their social structure is more like that of the ancient Earth species known as bees. The hive consists of a single Queen, the alpha female, and millions of drones and workers of both genders. Drones, such as my keepers, are intellectuals and warriors. Workers are servants, destined by their DNA to obey the commands of the drones.

While technically a drone, Champion Tsagadai was in a caste by himself. His official title was Queen's Champion, but he was more than her guard and defender. He was her mate. When the time was right, he would sire the egg that would become the next Tse-Tsunxhanaga queen. For him to have spoken directly to one of my keepers was a distinct honor.

Tserig recovered first and, raising his head, broke the reverent silence. "You bring us great honor, Tsagai. For Champion Tsagadai to speak to one of us..." he paused, waving his anterior antennae, "...it is beyond expectation."

Tsila nodded his great head. "We are merely keepers of a lowly human. We are unworthy of his notice."

Tsagai straightened to his full and considerable height. "It is because of the human that the Champion spoke to me. Her people did what no other species has done: they destroyed one of our flagships. We are to spare no expense in making Zara's speech intelligible. The Queen and her Champion have plans for our little human."

2

_____

I sat alone in an exo-bubble on the surface of a dead moon, far from the home world of the noble Tse-Tsunxhanaga hive. My bubble contained a recycling unit to ensure my supply of breathable air, a food processor, a toilet, atmospheric controls so that I would neither bake in the harsh sunlight nor freeze in the interstellar night, and my educational unit. I wore nothing but the enhancement collar that allowed me to speak intelligibly. The exo-bubble also contained an emergency beacon tuned to a frequency known to be monitored by the vermin who were the species of my birth.

Were I not bait, I would have enjoyed sitting in my bubble under the moon's open sky. The brightness of the stars, not to mention their sheer numbers, enchanted me. But, as always in my captivity with the Tse-Tsunxhanaga, my pleasure or displeasure was not a concern. I was merely a means to an end.

Champion Tsagadai and the queen's war council hoped to lure a human ship to my rescue. They wished to ensnare the ship and its crew in order to learn how my vastly inferior species had managed to destroy their flagship at the Battle for Absaroka.

I prayed that I would die alone on that harsh and lifeless moon, under those beautiful but uncaring stars.

The speaker on my beacon crackled to life, and I heard a human voice for the first time since my captivity began. "This is *USL Odyssey*. We have received your distress signal. Respond if you are able."

My heart sank. The emergency beacon had no microphone. I had no way to speak a warning. I could only observe as the system automatically pinged out a response.

"Confirmation received. A rescue party is on the way."

The trap had been sprung. I could do nothing but wait and observe the outcome of the confrontation between my people and the hive which had raised me.

All too soon, a shuttle craft landed on the barren surface of the dead moon. An exterior portal opened and three beings emerged. I knew from my educational device that they wore exo-suits, skin-tight protective gear that included a helmet designed to provide breathable air while allowing maximum visual and auditory acuity.

I had no such gear.

The three humans approached. The exo-suits molded so closely to their body contours that even I, who had such limited experience with my species, could tell that two were male and one was female.

Unfamiliar emotions roiled through me. I'd read about such feelings on my educational device, but had rarely experienced them. The thunder in my ears and palpitations of my heart told me I was excited to meet others of my kind, while the swooping sensation in my core and the prickles of tears in my eyes spoke of sorrow...and perhaps shame.

I was the bait who unwillingly lured these three, and very likely all of their shipmates, to their doom.

I knelt in my exo-bubble and awaited their fate...as well as my own.

The female approached while her companions held back, scanning the horizon with weapons drawn. She placed a small, black-and-silver device on the surface of my bubble and spoke.

"Do you understand Standard?" she asked. Her voice buzzed slightly, but was pleasant to my ears. Not the harsh clicking and humming of the Tse-Tsunxhanaga language, but soft and melodious.

I stared at her in wonder, longing for her to speak again.

She knelt on the dusty ground, placed her hand on the bubble, and leaned as close to me as her helmet and the exo-bubble would allow. "Can you understand me?"

Her meaning broke through my enchantment with the sound of her voice, and I nodded my head. "I understand."

My own voice sounded creaky and hoarse; disuse and constant practice with the clicks and sub-glottal stops of my captors' language had caused my native tongue to languish.

She smiled, and I was awash in emotion. This female had come to help me. She didn't deserve what was about to happen. My mind raced as I tried to piece together words and phrases from my educational device that would convey her danger.

"Flee," I said, rising upright on my knees. "Leave this place before you are trapped. Ignore me. I am bait."

My voice strengthened with each word I spoke, the pitch rising as my emotions tainted the content.

Before she could answer, or I could explain further, Tse-Tsunxhanaga warriors swarmed from the underground bunker where they kept watch.

My would-be rescuer sprang to her feet, drew her weapon, and shouted a warning to her companions. The two males laid down cover fire as they raced to their shuttle craft. When the shuttle doors closed and its engines fired, the female spoke again.

"Captain Fielding to *Odyssey*. I have activated a force field and am adhered to the subject's exo-bubble. Deploy the tractor beam. We are in imminent danger. Prepare for an emergency jump."

Before I could take a breath to speak, my bubble— and the human attached to it— lifted from the moon's surface. I watched in awe as the Tse-Tsunxhanaga warriors dwindled to mere specks and my rescuer and I flew through the upper atmosphere, into the black clarity of space, where we were drawn toward a vast deep space vessel.

I had never seen an interstellar craft.

I had been caged and taken aboard the Tse-Tsunxhanaga vessel like so much cargo. No one had been concerned with my experience. When we arrived at the desired location, the drones had simply placed my cage in a shuttle craft and then transferred me to the exo-bubble on the surface.

The *Odyssey* was immense, so shiny it sparkled against the backdrop of distant stars.

But a second sparkling craft emerged from what I guessed to be the mouth of a light-speed tunnel. My captors' ship had arrived. My rescue, though sweet, had been too short to be of consequence.

My rescuer and I were drawn into an open aperture on the *Odyssey* and deposited upon a dark metallic deck. As soon as the aperture closed behind the returning shuttle craft, before she even deactivated the force field adhering her to my bubble, the female shouted an order. "Fielding here. Shields up! Jump to light-speed. Now!"

The floor beneath the thin skin of my bubble thrummed with energy. The female joined her companions as they emerged from the shuttle, and all three removed their helmets.

They stood at ease, but the edges of my vision darkened and I felt as though my whole body were being squeezed in the pincers of my Tse-Tsunxhanaga keepers. My breath expelled in a *whoosh*...

...and then all returned to normal.

The female stared at me, a small frown wrinkling the skin between her brows. "You're unfamiliar with the jump to light-speed?"

I rose to my full height and returned her stare, noting that her male companions turned their eyes away from my body. "I am unfamiliar with all things human, including your light-speed engines," I said. "I have been captive to the noble Tse-Tsunxhanaga since I was very young."

"The what?" she asked, confused by the pronunciation my enhancement collar required.

I closed my eyes, imagining Champion Tsagadai's rage at having lost not only the *Odyssey*, but his bait as well. A bubble of...delight?...welled up in my core. For once, my captors had been outwitted. By lowly humans. And I had been part of their failure. I relished the knowledge.

Opening my eyes, I clarified the term for the captain. "You call them *Bug-Eyes*."

3

———

*C*aptain Fielding had a young female escort me to the medical bay, where a doctor evaluated my health. When I was released, the female took me to what she described as *my quarters*. I was certain I had misunderstood her intent. The enclosure was far more spacious than my container coupled with the training center where all three of my keepers studied me and conducted their research.

She explained that the three sections were a bedroom (for sleeping), a combination living area and kitchen (for entertaining and eating), and a toilet for relieving myself and ritual cleansing. The bed fascinated me. I'd never had more than a mat on the floor and a thin blanket, a concession to the fragile nature of my pitiful, non-chitinous body.

The female remained, having been instructed to help me clothe myself. She didn't believe I needed assistance, but my complete bafflement as to what to do with the pieces of cloth she provided soon convinced her.

Once I was cleansed, groomed, and suitably clothed, she escorted me to yet another enclosure, this one containing a long white table surrounded by ten fixtures I recognized as chairs. I continued to bless my keepers for allowing me to retain my instructional device. The knowledge I had gleaned over the years was proving invaluable in my new surroundings. The enclosure had white walls and floor (I wondered if they might be the plasteel I had read about), and one long wall contained indentations I thought might be windows, but they were also covered in white.

On one short wall was what I imagined to be a holoscreen showing images of a green and blue planet. I approached it, fascinated. The images shifted from— were those trees?— a forest to mountains—I'd seen mountains on my device—to a planet hanging against the backdrop of interstellar space.

I had never seen such beauty. The size of the holoscreen magnified the grandeur of what I'd experienced on my small handheld device. I couldn't imagine what it would be like to experience those wonders in person.

The door *whooshed* open behind me, and I turned to face Captain Fielding.

She smiled. "Well, you certainly clean up nicely."

I glanced down at myself. I felt... foreign... with my body encased in cloth, but I also felt warm and...protected. My young escort had named each piece as she helped me put it on. I wore soft knit leggings of the color known as navy blue, a long-sleeved tunic, also knit, in russet, and soft leather boots. I believe their color could best be described as *fawn*. She had seemed distressed by the scars on my body, and by my shaved head, but assured me that the soft blue scarf she'd wound around my head accented the color of my eyes.

Silence rang through the room, until my escort nudged me.

Ah. I was expected to respond.

I thought back to the conversational records I'd read on my device, and said, "Thank you."

Captain Fielding nodded. She wore what I now recognized

as a uniform, blue and silver. Like my escort, her head had not been shaved. She wore her dark hair in a knot at the base of her skull. She gestured toward the chairs and my escort moved to sit upon one.

I watched how she folded herself into the space, and, licking my lips, made an attempt to do likewise. Soft padding cushioned my buttocks and supported my spine, I glanced sideways and saw that my arms could also be supported by cushioned comfort.

I closed my eyes and relished the...perhaps the word *decadence* applied?

Everything on this ship felt soft to me. How could such creatures have defeated a flagship of the mighty Tse-Tsunxhanaga? I shuddered to think how easily they would have been crushed had the captain not managed to jump to light-speed so expediently.

Captain Fielding's voice pulled me from my thoughts.

"I have your initial medical reports here, Zara. I believe you told Dr. Jansson that was your name. May I call you Zara?"

I opened my eyes and nodded.

"Dr. Jansson finds you malnourished, but otherwise in reasonable health." She paused and swiped forward a few screens on the device she held. "He also commented on the number of scars on your torso. Were you tortured?"

I frowned, trying to place the word in context. "I am unsure of your meaning," I replied. "My keepers discovered that my skin tore easily when they were forced to scrape the unsightly tendrils—I think you call it hair—from my body. They found me fragile and assumed I was defective. They continued to study me since I was their only test subject, but they could not imagine that a species as weak as I could possibly endure the rigors of space exploration."

Captain Fielding's eyebrows rose and the skin on her face

flushed an interesting color. "I see." She swallowed, and I watched the play of muscles on her throat. Fascinating. "Do you remember how old you were when you were taken captive?"

I concentrated, accessing the few memories I had of the time before the Tse-Tsunxhanaga. "I was four Earth-years old when the hive invaded my colony. All were destroyed except me."

My guide gasped, and I glanced at her. The expression on her face made my heart pound. Her already pale face was even more pallid, and the expression in her eyes...

I could not interpret its meaning.

Captain Fielding asked, "Do you remember the name of the colony?" and I turned my attention back to her. The calmness of her tones and her straightforward questions were soothing. Emotions were too new. I did not understand them, did not know what they meant. Questions I could answer; had been answering as long as I had existed.

"I do not know. I have often wondered, once I matured enough to understand that not all places are the same, but I am not sure I ever knew. I was too young to be concerned. It was simply my colony. My home."

"I understand." Captain Fielding looked down at her device. Fleetingly, I wondered if she might be avoiding my gaze. But my experience was too limited to judge.

When she again met my eyes, it was with calm assurance. "When we spoke on that moon, you told me to flee, that you were bait. Why did you say that? Why warn me away? Wouldn't it have been safer to stay silent?"

I lowered my eyes to my hands, where they rested on the soft padding of the chair, and composed my response. "I have dreamed of meeting my people, though my keepers assured me that my species were vermin to be exterminated from the universe.

"When I understood that I was to be used as bait to trap

additional humans for continuing study, I wished to die. My existence has been unpleasant. I did not wish anyone else to share it, though I desperately longed for the company of my own kind."

I raised my gaze to hers and held it. "I did not believe you would be able to escape my captors. I never dreamed you would rescue me as well."

Her eyes brightened, seeming to fill with fluid, possibly tears. I had not cried in many years. The exercise was unprofitable, as it would only cause my keepers to do intensive, painful research on my eyes to try to determine the cause of the moisture.

"I thank you, on behalf of myself and my crew. We'll never know if we could've battled our way out, but our experience with the Bug-Eyes argues against it. Can you tell me why they chose to use you now, and not years ago?"

"Years ago they did not consider humans a threat," I answered, "but recently their opinion of you has escalated. Humans destroyed one of their flagships at the Battle of Absaroka."

Her gaze sharpened and she leaned forward in her chair, placing her arms on the table. "How do you know that?"

I shrugged. "My keepers doubted my intelligence."

She frowned, but remained quiet.

"Because my vocal apparatus is unable to produce their language intelligibly, they think me stupid. I understand them perfectly; I simply could not respond well, until recently. Because of that, they often discussed events in my presence. Things they might not have said if they had known I understood."

"What changed recently?"

"They developed the enhancement collar."

"The one you were wearing when we found you?"

"Yes."

"Where is it now?"

"The doctor removed it when he examined me."

She turned her attention to my guide. "Ensign Walker, go to the medical bay and secure that collar."

My guide jumped to her feet and raced to the door. "At once, sir."

When the door *whooshed* closed behind my guide, Captain Fielding rose, walked around the table and sat beside me. I swiveled my chair to face her and met her gaze. She studied my eyes with an intensity I had never experienced, and I struggled to remain still, to not squirm under that scrutiny.

She leaned forward and held out her hand. I frowned at it, sliding my gaze to her face. "Take it," she murmured. "Touch your hand to mine."

I laid my palm on hers, my flesh tingling at the warmth of another human's touch.

"I want you to understand something, Zara," she said, and I raised my eyes from our linked hands to her face. "You are not weak, and you are not stupid. You have survived, alone, on an alien world. That alone speaks of your strength and your intelligence. More than that, you are brave. You showed your courage when you warned me away without concern for your own safety."

She paused and tightened her fingers around mine. My soul glowed with her praise.

"The Bug-Eyes have continually underestimated us. Both you as an individual, and humanity as a whole. They will regret allowing us to take you back."

Her words puzzled me. "But they didn't..."

"They thought to trap us, but they underestimated you. They failed to take your courage and compassion into consideration. They also underestimated us, both our people and the capabilities of our ship. Finally, they failed to understand and value the treasure that you are."

Her meaning escaped me. "I do not see how I can be a treasure."

She grinned and released my hand. "I know you don't. You've been undervalued for as long as you can remember. But, if you will consent to help your people, I can guarantee you will be treated as royalty. You will be a queen among us."

Queen. That was a word I understood.

"I have no wish to rule humans."

"No, you wouldn't, and you won't. What I mean to convey is that you will be valued for your knowledge, for the insight you can provide. You not only understand the Bug-Eye language, you understand their culture. If you will help us, we can find a way to share this universe. Hopefully without extermination on either side."

I cocked my head and studied her. "I have a choice?"

She nodded, her expression grave. "You do. You have been a captive long enough." She stared past my shoulder. "We desperately need your knowledge, but I will not allow you to be forced. If you will explain what you know of the collar and will work with one of our linguists while we travel, I will personally put you ashore on an amenable colony before we reach Earth and I will ensure that no records remain of where you landed."

I stood and walked to the holoscreen, watching the images play while I considered.

"Are all humans like you and the doctor and the ensign?"

"The *Odyssey* has an excellent crew, but no, not all humans are alike. There are good people who are brave and true and strive to do the right, the honorable thing. But there are also bad people, and a lot more who are neither good nor bad, simply doing the best they can with what they have been given."

"I understand." I turned away from the beautiful images and

walked back to Captain Fielding. "I have not known you, or any human, long, but I trust you. If you think I can help, then I will."

I held out my hand, and she grasped it firmly.

"I have dreamed of finding my people too long to desert them now."

Without releasing either my hand or my gaze, Captain Fielding activated her comm. "Bridge, this is Captain Fielding. Set our course for Earth, by the fastest route possible."

She laid her free hand on my shoulder and squeezed. "Welcome home, Zara."

My heart sang at her words. I was home!

COPYRIGHT

THE LOST COLONY

$\mathcal{L}$ ieutenant Nick Adams strode across the carefully trimmed green lawns of the Headquarters of the Universal Star League. Located in the teeming city of New Atlantis on Earth's North American continent, the white marble and glass edifice glistened in the morning sun. Twenty stories tall, the building's footprint was immense, housing as it did the administrative offices of the Fleet, the Academy, and Nick's own service, Military Intelligence.

He jogged up the wide marble steps leading to the main entrance, his leather boots beating a clean, crisp rhythm against the stone. The gleaming glass doors *whooshed* open at his approach and he made his way briskly to the glide that would take him to Lieutenant Commander Popescu's office on the twelfth floor.

His superior officer had a new assignment for him, one she wouldn't trust to the USL's highly secure and very effective communications system. No, he'd been ordered to report in person this morning to receive a briefing on a complex and confidential assignment.

Excitement buzzed in his brain and sizzled through his

blood. Adventure was afoot... and he was definitely the man for the job.

Whatever it was.

Nick had graduated top of his class from the Academy a few months earlier. He knew himself to be brilliant, insightful, and diabolically cunning. His academic record proved him to be the most able analyst USL had ever trained. Now it was up to him to prove himself in the field, which he intended to do quickly and efficiently.

After all, he was the best. If Nick Adams couldn't see a pattern or discern a motive, then it didn't exist.

Jumping off the glide, Nick strode across the thick, USL blue carpet, past old-fashioned oak doors set in plasteel walls disguised as dark green painted plaster panels with oak wainscoting. Stopping in front of the door labeled *Lieutenant Commander Elena Popescu, Military Intelligence*, Nick tugged his USL blue uniform jacket straight and brushed imaginary lint from the silver USL insignia and lieutenant's bars.

Satisfied that his appearance was in good order, he tucked his cap under his arm and knocked.

"Enter."

Nick opened the door, stepped through into a small, but neat office, boasting a large desk in front of a floor-to-ceiling view wall, a pair of visitor chairs, and a tall potted plant that might be some form of palm. Closing the door with a satisfying snap, he came to attention and saluted, calling out, "Sir. Lt. Nick Adams, reporting as ordered."

LCdr. Popescu, a petite woman in a neatly pressed uniform with her dark hair drawn into a sleek knot at the nape of her neck, glanced up from the document she was studying on a holoscreen embedded in the surface of her twenty-first century walnut desk. Nick felt sure the piece of furniture was actually made of plasteel. Lieutenant commanders weren't high enough up the food chain to rate real wood... even in Military Intelligence.

"At ease, Lieutenant Adams. Take a seat," she said, indicating one of the two dark wood, padded chairs facing her desk.

"Thank you, Commander." Nick folded himself into the seat, but did not relax his vigilance.

LCdr. Popescu blanked the holoscreen and leaned forward on her forearms, hands clasped. "What I have to tell you is not to be discussed outside this office."

Nick nodded, his pulse rate increasing.

"Captain Caren Fielding of the *USL Odyssey*, a deep space exploratory vessel, has delivered an extraordinary asset to MI." She paused, studying Nick's face. Satisfied with what she saw, she continued. "Vice Admiral Zhou has assigned the asset to our section, though other sections, including linguistics, will have regular access to her."

Nick's interest piqued. A female asset. With information valuable to linguistics. Interesting.

"You will interview the asset, determine her native colony, and, if possible, her identity."

"Excuse me?"

Popescu smiled. "So you haven't heard any scuttlebutt regarding this asset?"

Nick shook his head, frowning. "No, Commander. Should I?"

"No, Lieutenant, you shouldn't," she said, relaxing back into her chair. "But, given your reputation, I thought if anyone had ferreted it out, it would be you."

Nick wasn't sure whether to be complimented or insulted, but he kept his expression carefully neutral, and nodded, waiting for her to give him more information.

LCdr. Popescu continued, "The asset, a young woman known as Zara, has been a captive of the Bug-Eyes since early childhood. As far as she knows, she is the only survivor of a colony that was attacked and destroyed when she was about four years old."

"A Bug-Eye captive?" Nick blurted, his eyes widening, pulse thundering. "Are you sure?" He fought to bring himself under control, schooled his expression, and apologized for his outburst. "Sorry, Sir."

"That's quite all right, Lieutenant. Zara represents a huge question mark to the entire USL, which is why we have been assigned to research and check her story. She was young enough at the time of her capture that she has no idea which colony she belonged to."

Nick's mind whirled with questions. Some he would ask this Zara in his interview, others he would have to discover for himself.

"And Capt. Fielding believed her story?" he asked.

"She found no reason not to," Popescu responded. "The *Odyssey* rescued Zara from a remote moon where she had been placed by the Bug-Eyes." She paused, watching his reaction, and seemingly satisfied, continued. "The young woman was used as bait. Only Zara's warning and Capt. Fielding's fast action saved the *Odyssey*."

Nick frowned, leaning forward. "I've never heard of the Bug-Eyes attempting to take captives before."

"Which is probably why their trap was so deficient."

"But why make the attempt now?"

"According to Zara, the Bug-Eyes are concerned over the loss of their flagship at the Battle for Absaroka. They believed their new weapons would render them invulnerable to our species." She smiled, though the expression was hardly a happy one. "We've risen in their esteem. They want to know more about us and our capabilities."

LCdr. Popescu rose, and Nick followed her lead. Walking

around her desk, she extended her hand to him, he clasped it firmly and, after a single brisk shake, released it.

"Good luck, Lt. Adams. My aide will assist you in scheduling your first meeting with Zara. Be discreet, and be careful in your dealings with her. Remember, if what she tells us is true, this young woman has had very little contact with humans. She is unfamiliar with our customs and our history. You may find her very difficult to read."

"Understood, sir," Nick replied. "And, sir?"

"Yes, Lieutenant?"

"Thank you for trusting me with this mission."

LCdr. Popescu nodded and motioned to the door. "You are dismissed, Lt. Adams."

2

Two days later Nick Adams entered one of the posh apartments in the headquarters building that were kept in ready for visiting planetary dignitaries. One had been set aside for the asset's use. When the female ensign assigned to act as her aide ushered him into the living area, he noted appreciatively that Zara had been given one of the best suites. Rose-brown carpet so plush his boots sank into the pile, tasteful furnishings that spoke of old world elegance, actual paintings on the walls instead of the more standard changeable holoscreens, and floor-to-ceiling windows that looked out on the great forested park behind the gleaming edifice.

Someone wanted to ensure this woman's comfort and contentment among her own people.

Nick understood the impulse.

He'd spent the intervening time refreshing his knowledge of the Bug-Eye incursions into human occupied space in general, and the Battle for Absaroka in particular. The enemy had chosen that lightly populated, and to its mind lightly defended, planet to experiment with a new and deadly weapon. Only the intuitive grasp of the situation on the part of the planetary war chief, coupled with her willingness to sacrifice herself for her people had won the day. Absaroka had lost a valiant warrior, but the planet had survived to provide valuable information to USL Command.

That defeat had also led to Zara's recovery, and from the reports Nick had read, her knowledge of the Bug-Eyes and their social systems was unparalleled, and therefore priceless.

He had read Capt. Fielding's report on Zara's rescue and their subsequent interactions. And he had viewed the holograms of her initial intake screening. The young woman had arrived on the *Odyssey* naked, bruised, and scarred. She had also been entirely hairless: her head shaved, her eyebrows and lashes removed, and her pubic ridge denuded.

Nick, who prided himself on his emotional detachment and a certain worldly acceptance of the times he found himself in, had been appalled. Zara might be a spy, brainwashed by the enemy and allowed to be rescued in order to wreak havoc among her own kind, but there was no doubt she'd been captive, poorly treated, and tortured.

Even with advance preparation, Nick failed to stifle a gasp and the automatic reaction of turning his eyes away when she entered the room. Flushing and swearing silently, he mastered himself and came to attention.

"Lt. Nick Adams, ma'am. LCdr. Popescu has asked me to assist you in finding your identity."

Zara smiled, a wistful expression that did nothing to diminish the power of her presence. For even before she uttered a word, the strength of her personality pervaded the room. She was casually dressed in dark leggings, a pale green tunic, and a paisley scarf of muted colors. Her feet were bare. Of average height, perhaps five-six or five-seven, she was slender and lithe and bore herself with dignity.

Nick wondered where the captive had learned that innate self-respect.

Her hair had begun to grow out, honey blonde and perhaps two inches in length, the bones of her facial structure were fine, her eyes a clear blue.

She would have been a beautiful woman were it not for the scars crisscrossing her face and every other portion of exposed skin. Their evidence even carried into her soft hair, causing streaks of premature white amid the honey blonde strands.

"Please be seated, Lt. Adams. I have been briefed on your assignment and am ready to assist in any way I can."

Nick forced his eyes away from his scrutiny of her person and met her gaze. "Thank you, Zara. May I call you Zara?" He selected a comfortable looking padded chair and sat.

"You may," she said quietly, seating herself on a creamy blue sofa across from him. "You may also continue your scrutiny. I am accustomed to being observed."

"Forgive my rudeness," he said, flushing yet again. "I didn't mean to offend."

"No offense was offered," she said, inclining her head, "and none was taken. I have learned that humans find my appearance... disconcerting. I accept that fact."

Nick released the breath he'd been holding and nodded. "You were tortured, then."

She frowned, her newly grown eyebrows drawing together. "Tortured?" she asked. "Not intentionally, no."

Nick's eyes widened in surprise, his own eyebrows shooting toward his hairline. "Then how..."

"Forgive me," she said, thoughtfully. "I am still learning to interpret your meanings, to understand your ways. Perhaps I am mistaken. Does torture not require a certain malice? An intent to do harm to the person undergoing the torture?"

Nick nodded. "Yes. Those things were not present when you were... mistreated?"

Her full, lovely lips curved upward in the smallest of smiles. "No. My keepers, while not precisely concerned with my comfort, were nonetheless making an honest effort to care for me. Being a species with a nearly indestructible exoskeleton, they found my tender skin mystifying."

"Then all the scars on your body..."

"Came from their attempts to cleanse me and make me presentable. They were horrified by how easily my skin tore, by the dark colors that would appear for no apparent reason."

"For no apparent reason?" Nick echoed, unbelievingly.

She laughed at his confusion. "Certainly for no reason they understood. The taps which caused me to bruise wouldn't even be felt by one of their kind."

Nick closed his eyes. He couldn't imagine a small child enduring the amount of abuse this woman must have borne.

"I am sorry for your suffering, Zara," he said quietly, searching for a question that would move the interview to a new topic. He asked the first thing that occurred. "You speak standard very well for someone who has been away from it so long. May I ask how you kept the language fresh in your mind?"

Her expression brightened. "Of course! It was my educational device." At his blank look, she jumped to her feet, moving quickly away from the sitting area. "Wait. I'll show you."

When she returned a few moments later, she handed Nick a small tablet of the type he himself had used as a child.

"The warrior who captured me found this in my home. He gave it to my keepers thinking it might be of use in determining my care." She gazed fondly at the device, then raised her eyes to meet Nick's. "It was useless to them since they understood neither our writing nor our spoken language, but it was invaluable to me."

"And they allowed you to keep it?" he asked, amazed at the stupidity of a species that the USL considered highly intelligent.

Zara shrugged and resumed her seat. "It calmed me, and they thought it contained no more than nursery songs and pictures of my home world, neither of which threatened them."

"But this unit contains far more than that," Nick objected, studying her intently. "If it's similar to the one I used, it contains a data base and courses of study to prepare a student for university."

"Exactly," she said, her expression shrewd. "But I never allowed my keepers to see it as more than a toy, a reminder of my lost life."

His respect for her intelligence and cunning increased exponentially.

"Capt. Fielding's report stated that you can both understand and speak the Bug-Eye language."

"Not precisely," she said. "I understand their language and can translate it accurately, but I can only speak it intelligibly when wearing the collar my keepers designed for me."

"Of course," he said, remembering the notation in the report. "I believe we have scientists attempting to reverse engineer the device now." She nodded, and he continued, "You're also working with Linguistics to teach our best people to understand and translate."

"Correct, though it is a slow process. They would learn faster through immersion, though I wouldn't wish my captivity on anyone."

He nodded, and felt for the test packet in his pocket. It was time to end this interview, but he needed a DNA sample before he could move to the next phase of his investigation.

"I know the doctor on the *Odyssey* took blood samples, but I'd like to collect a fresh cheek swab to test your DNA." He pulled the packet from his pocket and held it out for her inspection. "Will you permit this?"

She stared at the packet, but didn't take it, frowning slightly, puzzled by the request. "For what purpose?"

"Your DNA will help us identify the colony you came from. All colonists are tested, their DNA recorded. Those records are kept in the administrative offices of the USL's Colonial Bureau. Even if you were born on the colony, your DNA should help us identify your parents, who are undoubtedly listed in the Bureau's records."

"I see," she said, nodding. "This... *swab*... may allow you to tell me who my parents were?"

Nick nodded. "Better than that, it may help us determine if you have any living relatives."

She gasped. "Living relatives?" Her complexion paled, and she closed her eyes. "Forgive me. I never considered that such a thing might be possible.

Crap, Nick thought.

"I'm sorry," he said quickly. "I shouldn't have gotten your hopes up. It's unlikely I'll find anyone in your family still living."

She opened her eyes and laughed, the first truly happy sound he'd heard. "Don't worry, Lt. Adams. It's very hard to disappoint someone who has learned to always expect the worst." She leaned forward. "By all means, take your sample."

3

ick studied the holoscreen in the research carrel he'd been assigned in the Colonial Bureau's Hall of Records. The carrel was actually a small enclosure with glass walls that could be blanked for privacy. The charcoal gray plasteel work surface gleamed in the soft, even lighting and the ergonomically correct chair supported his body efficiently, if not precisely comfortably.

He'd inserted Zara's DNA profile into computer system, and the vast database now searched for matches, both exact and familial. While the system worked, Nick ran a parallel program searching for colonies that had failed to report for more than a decade. Since regular reports were not a requirement for colonization, he doubted this particular enquiry would be fruitful. Colonies often ignored the Bureau unless a catastrophic event forced them to request USL assistance.

As expected, his search returned dozens of possibilities. He needed more details. Before he left Zara's apartment, he'd examined her educational device, hoping that the manufacturing stamp would provide a clue as to its colony of origin, but that too came up empty. The tablet had been manufactured on Excelsior, like almost all of the Fleet's electronic equipment, and shipped to the Colonial Bureau at New Atlantis on Earth. From there it had been added to stores and loaded onto a colony ship.

The Bureau kept track of lots and crates, but not of individual units.

The only meaningful information Nick had to go on was Zara's DNA, and that search could run for days.

He'd just decided to take a walk and find the Bureau's cafeteria, when the holoscreen lit and two 3-D images appeared in the air above the work surface. The images revolved slowly to allow viewing from all angles. Nick sat back down, staring at the couple before fingering their data onto a second holoscreen beside their images.

The woman strongly resembled Zara... an unscarred Zara, but the slant of her eyes and the shape of her nose weren't quite right.

Nick glanced at the man. Yes. His eyes and nose matched Zara's more closely.

The woman's hair was platinum blonde; the man's a light chestnut; Zara's honey blonde a blend of the two. Both her parents were young, healthy specimens in their holo-depictions. Vibrant young lives that had been cut far too short.

Satisfied with his visual review of the images, Nick turned to the written report.

Annalise Cole and Holger Martinsen had been married less than a year when they boarded the colony ship *USL Hope's Horizon* bound for Kapteyn 5. Holger, from Earth's Scandinavian region, and Annalise, from Moon Base Alpha, had met in New Atlantis when both completed internship years in the Colonial Bureau's recruitment division. They'd intended to recruit others to colonize, but had decided to take the plunge themselves.

A fatal decision for themselves, and life-changing for their daughter, as it turned out.

Copying the images and data for his report, Nick blanked the holoscreens and began a new search for information about the colony on Kapteyn 5.

Before he left the Hall of Records, Nick recorded every scrap of information available on the USL colony designated Terranova: population, climate, geophysical characteristics, even a complete analysis of survey data, including soil and mineral compositions. He also found a few records of births (written only, no DNA had been transmitted) that had occurred during the colony's first two years. Including one for a baby girl born to Holger and Annalise Martinsen, Sara Elise Martinsen.

Nick had completed his mission. He knew Zara's identity, Sara Elise Martinsen, and her native colony, Terranova on Kapteyn 5. Having found her birth record, he even knew her age. Zara was twenty-four standard years old. She had spent twenty years in captivity.

But it was what he didn't know that worried him.

Why had the Bug-Eyes destroyed that particular colony? The aggressive aliens had originally invaded USL space more than seventy years ago. The fleet had beaten them back. Barely, and at great cost… but they hadn't been heard from again until the Battle of Absaroka, nearly two years ago.

At least, the USL hadn't been aware of any further incursions.

Now it seemed that the Bug-Eyes had destroyed a human colony twenty years ago, and then retreated into their own region of space.

Why?

What, if anything, had Terranova done to threaten the aliens?

Nick had the feeling that when he reported to LCdr. Popescu tomorrow, his mission parameters would be expanded.

4

*N*ick arrived at LCdr. Popescu's office promptly at 0900. Her aide ushered him into the commander's office immediately. The door had barely closed behind him before Nick snapped to attention and saluted.

"Sir. Lt. Nick Adams, ready to report."

"At ease, Lieutenant." LCdr. Popescu stood with her back to the room, gazing out of the view wall. She turned, and motioning Nick into one of the visitor chairs, took her own place behind her desk. "That was fast work, Adams. I hadn't expected a report so soon. What have you learned?"

Nick handed her a printed copy of his full report, succinctly summing up his findings verbally.

LCdr. Popescu paged through the print-out as he spoke, nodding at the mention of Zara's name and colony. When he finished, she met his gaze. "And what was your impression of the asset?"

Nick relaxed into the chair. If the commander was asking his opinion, she'd found his report acceptable. "I found Zara compelling and believable," he said. "I'm sure the USL will request a full psychological work-up, but I found no reason not to accept her as what she claims to be... a captive who has been restored to her people."

Popescu nodded. "We are in agreement." She flipped a page in his report before asking, "What do you see as our next step, Lieutenant?"

Brushing a hand through his hair, Nick frowned. "I'd like to follow up on a few items that puzzle me."

"Such as?"

"Why the Bug-Eyes felt the need to destroy that particular colony, and why they felt the need to obtain a specimen for study. Nothing in my research indicates that the colony had any dealings with the aliens, and I didn't find any indication of particularly rich veins of valuable or unusual minerals."

He paused, shifted in his chair, and continued. "And taking captives for study is outside their prior dealings with humanity."

"I agree, those are puzzling points. What else?"

"I'd also like to follow up with a reference I found to a trader from Terranova. He seems to have been off-planet at the time of the attack. If he knew the colony had been eradicated, why didn't he report the loss? Why ignore the deaths of everyone he knew?

LCdr. Popescu frowned. "Excellent questions." She closed her eyes, tapping her lips with an index finger as she pondered. "Yes. Further inquiry is called for. Consider the resolution of these questions your next assignment: why Terranova; why take a captive; and who is this trader and what did he know?"

She stood and nodded toward the door. Nick stood as well, recognizing a dismissal when he saw one. Turning with military precision, he strode to the door.

"Lt. Adams," LCdr. Popescu called.

Nick paused and turned, one eyebrow raised in question. "Sir?"

"Well done."

"Thank you, sir." With a sharp salute, he left the lieutenant commander's office.

5
---

*N*ick went straight to his desk in the Office of Analysis and Decryption. His cubicle was neither spacious nor private, but the room was usually quiet as the analysts tended to become immersed in their various projects.

Opening his holoscreen, he moved directly into the information he'd gleaned on the Terranova trader. Soren Ivarrson, captain and sole owner of the registered trading vessel *Brisk Venture*. A quick records search found that the *Venture* had been docked on Optimus V at the estimated time of Zara's capture. Nick was able to trace the movements of Capt. Ivarrson and the *Venture* for another few weeks before both the vessel and the man disappeared.

Undaunted, Nick entered Ivarrson's DNA into the system and searched the Space Registry database (ownership records for all non-fleet spacefaring vessels), the Immigration database (records of change of citizenship from one colony to another), and the Inter-Colonial Crime Detection exchange (ICCD), USL's law enforcement database. If Ivarrson was still living, Nick would find the man.

Scrutinizing the records of Ivarrson's final recorded year,

Nick suspected that something had frightened the trader into going underground. The man could change his name and the *Venture's* registration, but he couldn't change his DNA. Fortunately for Ivarrson, DNA records were classified. Only a USL officer with sufficient clearance could access that data.

Nick's hunch proved correct when he found a DNA match to one Mitchell Preston, citizen of Proxima Prime, and captain of the *Lucky Fortune*. A little more digging, and Nick discovered that the *Lucky Fortune* was currently docked Earth-side, with her captain listed as berthing at the Spacefarer's Rest, a cheap lodging house in the spaceport district of... New Atlantis!

Grinning, Nick wiped his research and left the administration building. Jogging across the USL campus to his quarters, he breathed in the sweet smell of success along with fresh air scented by the nearby forest and beds of blooming spring flowers. New Atlantis maintained scrupulous standards when it came to scrubbing the air for noxious odors and pollutants. Gone were the bad old days when the atmosphere around major metropolitan cities was polluted with smog and industrial gases.

Breathing easily and excited by his progress, Nick palmed the door to his quarters and stepped inside. Quickly changing from his uniform to casual dark brown slacks, deep burgundy short-sleeved pullover shirt, and a stylish faux leather retro-bomber jacket, Nick reviewed the questions he intended to put to Ivarrson/Preston.

An hour later, Nick stood in the lobby of the Spacefarer's Rest. Accessing one of their intercom units, he buzzed Preston's berth. A bleary-eyed man in his early fifties appeared on the small holoscreen. His salt-and-pepper hair was disheveled and he sported a distinctly scruffy beard shadow.

"Preston," he answered, then peered at his screen. "Do I know you?"

"No, sir," Nick replied. "Sorry to disturb your rest. I was told you might be able to help me with a... well, a delicate proposition. Do you have time for a cup of java and some conversation?"

As Nick had hoped, the man's eyes lit at the mention of a delicate proposition.

"Sure. Just give me a minute to pull myself together."

"No problem. Shall we meet around the corner at the Helios Café?" Nick asked. "I'm buying, of course."

"Of course. I'll join you in a few." Preston ended the transmission.

Whistling tunelessly, Nick pushed his way through streets crowded with travelers and residents in many forms of dress from myriad colonies. He recognized the flowing, brightly colored garb of Cenatuarans, the elaborate, though drably colored, headdresses of Seti, and the distinctive wetsuits (so ill-advised in New Atlantis' warm climate) of the water dwellers of Aquarius. Other interesting, and odd to his eyes, folks mingled with the known, but the crowd moved along easily, people weaving purposefully toward their own destinations.

With little effort, Nick found the Helios Café, secured a two-top table, and ordered two cups of java. Coffee, real coffee brewed from beans grown from actual soil, wasn't available in the dives that served this district, but java was an acceptable alternative. The taste was unremarkable, but drinkable, and the non-alcoholic brew wouldn't dull the senses.

By the time the java was served, Preston had joined Nick. The man looked much better than his holo. He'd shaved, combed his hair, and dressed in a black tunic and pants. His expression, no longer sleep-fogged, was alert and interested.

"Mitch Preston," he said, extending his hand, "and you are?"

Nick shook the offered hand. "Nick Adams. Glad to meet you, Mr. Preston."

Preston nodded and took the seat opposite Nick. "What can I do for you, Adams?"

Nick picked up his cup of java and sipped, studying Preston over the rim. Taking his time, he replaced the cup on the table, and folded his hands.

"You can tell me why you changed your name, Capt. Ivarrson," he said quietly, but firmly, "and what you know about the destruction of Terranova."

The man flinched, the color draining from his face. He made a move to stand, but Nick grabbed his arm, refusing to let go when Preston tried to shake him off. After a moment, he settled back into his chair. Nick released him.

"Where did you hear that name? Either of those names?" Preston asked, a bit unsteadily.

"I've done my homework," Nick said with a shrug, lifting his cup and drinking again. Giving Preston the illusion of safely.

"Why do you care?"

"Let's just say it's an area of interest." Nick placed his cup back on the table and met the other man's gaze squarely. "Look, I'm not interested in revealing your identity. I just want to know what you know about Terranova... and whether or not what happened to that colony caused you to do a disappearing act."

Preston lowered his gaze, picked up his cup and sipped the steaming liquid. Placing the ceramic cup back on the table, he stared into the dark depths of the java. After a long moment, he nodded, raised his eyes, and met Nick's gaze.

"I was an original colonist on Terranova. Our colony ship carried my trading vessel in pieces in its hold. My trade charter was listed with the Colonial Office. I was just getting my trade runs established when the colony governor called me to her office."

Preston paused, sipped his java, eyes clouded with memory. Nick maintained his silence, unwilling to risk interrupting the flow of the man's thoughts.

"One of the miners had found an unknown ore. A substance

not listed in the original survey data. The planetary geologist had also been unable to identify it. The governor gave me a sample and the geologist's preliminary report and asked me to convey the packet to a more established world. The geologist suggested the university on Optimus V. He felt the staff there would have a good chance of telling us what we'd found."

Nick nodded. "I discovered that you'd been on Optimus V at the time we believe the attack was carried out. Were they able to identify the substance."

Preston shook his head. "I never delivered the sample." He swirled the remaining liquid in his cup, watching the motion intently. "I'd just docked when a distress call came in from Terranova, from the governor's office."

He looked up, his expression angry. "I heard them die. Heard the bugs unholy chittering. Heard her scream of pain, then the crackle of flames."

Nick glanced at his own cup. "You were close to the governor?"

"She was my wife."

Silence engulfed their small corner of the café. Beyond their table, people chatted and laughed, ate and drank. Utensils scraped ceramics, sounds of cooking and frying leaked from the kitchen. Waitstaff bustled between the tables.

Yet Nick and Preston sat enveloped by the ghosts of a long dead colony. A lost colony. One that only Soren Ivarrson, now Mitch Preston, and an asset named Zara had survived.

After an interminable moment, Nick spoke. "What happened to the sample and the report?"

Preston rubbed his eyes, as though he could erase the memory, the image of his wife's death from his mind. "I carried them around for a month or so while I made arrangements to disappear, then I stashed them on a planet and stayed as far away from their hiding place as I could."

"Why didn't you report the attack?"

"What good would it have done?"

A surge of anger thrummed through Nick's veins. He glared at the other man. "You might have saved other colonies. Didn't it occur to you that if the bugs had attacked once, they might attack again?"

Preston glared back. "Did they?" he asked. "Did anyone not of Terranova die?"

Nick's anger deflated. "No," he admitted. "But we might have looked for her sooner."

"What?" Preston's hand jerked, sloshing java onto the table top. "Who? Someone made it out alive?"

Nick silently cursed himself. He hadn't meant to mention Zara to this man.

"It's nothing," he said. "You wouldn't know her. She was just a child at the time."

"Who wouldn't I know?" Preston persisted. "How did she survive? I've seen what the bugs did to Terranova."

"Forget it," Nick said, louder than he'd intended. "Just tell me where that packet is and go back to your new life."

Preston reached across the table and grabbed Nick's jacket. "Listen, asshole! You searched me out. I didn't ask for this. Not for any of it. If you want that packet, you'll tell me who survived and how."

Nick jerked out of Preston's hold. "Come with me," he said, standing and dropping credits on the table to pay for the java. "I don't have the authority to make that call, but I know who does."

Preston's expression was grim, his color high, as he stood and nodded. "Lead on."

6

_____

*S*oren Ivarrson, also known as Mitch Preston, paled as he and Nick approached the massive USL administrative complex. "You didn't tell me you were with USL."

Nick gave him a sideways glance. "Would you have met me for java if I'd shown up in uniform?"

Preston grimaced. "Probably not."

The pair stopped on the marble steps leading to the main entrance.

"You don't have to go in," Nick said. "You can just give me the information on the sample and go back to your life."

Preston stared up at the marble and glass edifice and shook his head. "You've resurrected the ghosts," he said quietly. "I need to see this through. For Emma's sake."

Emma Preston. The colonial governor of Terranova. Of course. Ivarrson's choice of surname hadn't been random. He'd kept her alive in his name. The ghosts had never been far.

Nick nodded. "Let's get this deal done." He escorted Preston through security and up to the twelfth floor and LCdr. Popescu's office.

"Military intelligence?" Preston whispered as they approached Popescu's aide. Nick gave a curt nod.

Stopping before the aide's desk, he asked, "Is the commander in? I have an asset who'd like to make a request."

The young woman glanced at Nick, smiled, and then turned her attention to Preston. After a moment's study, she activated a voice-only communicator and said, "Commander, Lt. Adams and a civilian request a moment of your time."

Nick couldn't hear the response, but the aide said, "Of course, sir." Clicking the communicator off, the aide rose and escorted the men to LCdr. Popescu's door.

When the door closed behind them, Nick said, "Thank you for seeing us, sir."

Popescu stood behind her desk and waved the men forward. "Please, have a seat. Lieutenant, why are you out of uniform?"

Nick and Preston sat in the visitor chairs, while Popescu resumed her seat behind the desk, hands clasped on its surface.

"It seemed like the best tactic at the time, Commander," Nick said. "I didn't intend to end up in your office again quite so soon."

"Understood. Now, please introduce this gentleman and tell me what I can do for you."

"This is the trader I mentioned earlier. At the time of the incident, he was known as Soren Ivarrson. Now he goes by Mitch Preston."

Popescu quirked an eyebrow, but said mildly, "A pleasure, Mr. Preston."

"Preston, this is Lieutenant Commander Elena Popescu, Military Intelligence."

Preston inclined his head. "Ma'am."

"All right. Now that everyone knows each other, let me tell you what's happened." Nick gave his superior officer an abbreviated report on his research and his discussion with Preston.

When he finished, he added, "My apologies, sir. I had no right to allude to the asset. The comment just slipped out. And now Preston is refusing to cooperate further until I give him the identity of the other survivor."

"And tell me how he or she survived," Preston blurted out.

"I see," said Popescu. "Did your DNA research indicate kinship?"

"That doesn't matter," Preston said before Nick could reply. "We were a small colony. I was married to the governor. I knew everyone. I deserve to know who survived and how."

Nick ground his teeth, but kept silent. This was out of his hands.

Popescu leaned back, studying Preston, one long forefinger tapping her lower lip. After a moment, she activated her communicator and said, "Ensign Rand, please see if Zara is available for company."

"Zara?" Preston asked.

"You would know her as Sara Elise Martinsen," Popescu replied. "Lt. Adams only recently discovered her birth name."

"I don't understand."

"She was taken captive by the aliens," Popescu said, her voice calm and controlled. "One of our exploratory vessels rescued her a few months ago. We've been trying to piece together her history ever since."

Preston turned his attention on Nick. "You mean you didn't know about Terranova? Not until..."

"Not until I started researching Zara," Nick finished, giving Preston a haughty glare. "It would've been nice if you'd told us about it twenty years ago."

"That will do, Lt. Adams," Popescu said sharply. "What's done is done. Right now we need to find our way forward."

LCdr. Elena Popescu escorted Lt. Adams and Soren Ivarrson, now known as Mitch Preston, to Zara's quarters. As they neared the door to her rooms, Popescu stopped and fixed Preston with a commanding gaze.

"You will remember, Mr. Preston, that Zara was a captive for twenty years, for very nearly her entire life. You will control yourself. You will not cause her undue distress. You may not be under my command, but I will personally hold you accountable for your actions once we enter her rooms."

He nodded, though he looked a bit queasy. "I understand." Wiping his hands on his trousers and then raking his fingers through his hair, he said, "I'm ready."

Popescu nodded, placed a palm on the door panel, and announced herself. The door *whooshed* open.

When Nick followed the other two inside, he found Zara standing before the view wall, dressed in a gauzy blue lounge robe over deeper blue leggings and an ice white tunic. Her very short hair glowed against the backdrop of the deep green forest beyond the wall. Glancing from one to another of her guests, she appeared calm and relaxed, completely at home.

"LCdr. Popescu. Lt. Adams," she said, warmly. "Welcome. Please be at ease and introduce me to your friend."

Nick moved to the seating area, observing Preston as he did so. The man's face had blanched and his hands had begun to tremble. Nick was about to take his arm and guide him to a seat, when the man shook himself and stepped forward.

"Sara," he said, the hint of a smile curving his lips. "I'd know you anywhere. You look just like your mother." He stepped closer and held out his hand. "No, that's not quite true. I can see traces of Holger in your face as well."

Zara's calm fled. Her face paled and she stepped back a pace. "I'm sorry," she whispered. "Who are you?"

Preston dropped his hand to his side, shaking his head. "No.

Of course. I'm the one who should be sorry. You were little more than a baby the last time I saw you. You would've known me as Uncle Soren, but that was a long time ago."

She closed her eyes and lowered herself to the sofa, reaching out and finding the seat by feel. After a moment, she whispered, "Auntie Em." Opening her eyes, she studied the strange man. "Uncle Soren and Auntie Em."

His smile transformed his face, startling Nick with a glimpse of the young man he had once been. "Yes," he said with a laugh. "That's right."

"But how?"

LCdr. Popescu answered, filling the breathless gap. "Lt. Adams' research discovered another survivor of Terranova. Soren Ivarrson was a trader. He was off planet when the attack took place. He just happened to be on Earth for business. Actually, right here in New Atlantis. Lt. Adams was able to make contact today. When he learned of your existence, your uncle asked to see you."

Zara touched her face, her hair, and for the first time, Nick saw a hint of embarrassment about her appearance.

"And... and you recognize me?"

Soren smiled. "I recognize your resemblance to your mother." He glanced at the others, including them in his remarks. "I'm not an uncle by blood, but her mother, Annalise, and my Emma were best friends. They grew up together in the Lunar colony. Moon Base Alpha." He turned his attention back to Zara. "You look just like her, except around the eyes and nose." He grinned. "Those are pure Holger."

Zara rose, tears sparkling in her eyes. Soren rose as well. Cautiously, they moved toward each other, until like two magnets drawn irresistibly together, they were in each other's arms.

"Oh, my baby girl," Soren whispered. "I can't believe you're alive."

"You knew my parents," Zara said, her voice choked with emotion. "You recognize me... and know my name. Even I didn't know my name until a few days ago."

He kissed her very short and oddly streaked hair. "I know you. I know where you came from, and, if you'll let me, I'd like to be a surrogate father for you."

Tears streaked her face. "I don't even know what a father is," she sobbed. "Not really." She stepped out of his embrace and wiped her face. A smile blossomed, watered by her tears. "But I'd like you to help me find out."

Soren laughed. "I've never been a father," he admitted, his expression sobering. "I lost the chance when Emma died with Terranova." He inhaled deeply, regaining control, and let it out in a quick sigh. Then he smiled at her again. "Shall we figure it out together?"

She rushed back into his arms and buried her face against his tunic. "Deal!"

Popescu tapped Nick's shoulder, pulling his attention away from the drama unfolding before him. She motioned to the door, and he nodded. Standing, he followed her quietly from the room.

EPILOGUE

A week later, armed with the coordinates provided by Soren Ivarrson (for the Terranova trader had once again assumed his original identity), Lt. Nick Adams took a cruiser to recover the lost colony's mysterious ore sample and its attendant report. He hadn't yet discovered why the Bug-Eyes had targeted Terranova for destruction, but with that sample in hand, he felt certain the answer would be within his grasp. It was only a matter of time.

Zara and her colony were no longer lost.

He'd accomplished his mission, and— as always— he'd done it admirably.

COPYRIGHT

THE LOST COLONY
Copyright © 2020 by Debbie Mumford
Published by WDM Publishing
Cover and Layout copyright © 2020 by WDM Publishing
Cover design by WDM Publishing
Cover art copyright © Shad.off | Depositphotos.com

THE CASE OF THE GLITTERING HOARD

I slipped through the corridors as silent as a holographic image. I wasn't on a case, but a good detective hones her skills so they're ready when she needs them. At least, that's what Dad says, and since he's a real detective and I'm still a kid, I'll take his word for it.

It's not easy to be stealthy on a space station where you've spent your whole life. Even though my soft leather boots made no sound as I passed through purple sector's crowded marketplace, vendors who'd known me since infancy kept smiling and waving, a few even calling me by name.

"Good morning, Cinnamon," said Mr. Zitnik as he arranged fat, round loaves of fresh, crusty bread on the shelves of his stall. Tall and thin as one of Dad's fighting sticks, Mr. Zitnik always had a cookie or a tart ready for me. Today his dark eyes crinkled with suppressed laughter as he offered me a cinnamon sugar cookie.

I managed not to roll my eyes as I waved and said, "Thanks, Mr. Zitnik, but not today. I'm on a case." I wasn't, but the white lie kept me from accepting the cookie and allowing his good-natured teasing about my name. See, my dad actually calls me

Cinnamon Sugar Cookie. Now, I don't mind Dad referring to me as an overly sweet pastry, but I draw the line at casual acquaintances making the reference.

It all goes back to my birth. My mom, senior bridge officer for Space Station Zeta, has beautiful dark chocolate skin, while my dad, the station's chief security officer, is an utterly gorgeous golden hue. Since I'm a combination of the two, my skin tone is a spicy shade of cinnamon. That's where I got my name. Dad took one look at me and said, "She's perfect, Maria. Our own little cinnamon sugar cookie."

"Ahh," Mr. Zitnik said, replacing the cookie on its tray. "I wouldn't want to interfere with official business. Good hunting, little one."

I melted into the morning crowd making a mental note to use a disguise if I ever really needed to follow someone. Too many people knew me too well. I'd just managed to perfect my stealthy gait when my wrist link pinged. Several shoppers glanced my direction.

Mental note number two: silence your wrist link when tailing a suspect.

I gave up on stealth and strode boldly toward Trigger's Exotic Creature Emporium as I activated my wrist link. A tiny 3-D version of my best friend Sammy appeared above the link.

"Where are you?" she asked, minuscule fists on itty-bitty hips. "I've been here for ages!"

"Don't exaggerate," I said, picking up my pace. "I'm only a couple of minutes late."

"Fine. I was early," she admitted, "but you're still late."

"Almost there," I said and deactivated the connection. Sammy's tiny form winked out of existence. I swung around a decorative planter of Andolian fern trees, stepped up behind Sammy, and tapped her shoulder.

"Surprise! I'm here."

She jumped and whirled at the same time—a move I'm sure her Kendo instructor would've been proud of—and glared at me. "Why can't you ever just walk into my field of vision and say 'hello' like a normal person?"

I shrugged. "Where's the fun in that?"

Her glare morphed into a grudging grin and she grabbed my arm. "Come on. Mom said I could have a pet for my birthday and I want to check out the puppies."

This time I didn't bother to suppress an eye-roll. Puppies? Of all the exotic critters available at Trigger's, Sammy wanted to play with plain old Earth-normal puppies? My best friend had no imagination, no sense of adventure.

While Sammy cooed over the various breeds of available puppies, I examined the emporium's more unusual offerings. I smiled wistfully at a display of fluffy little Inarians. My previous best friend, Lando Maxon, had owned one of the hamster-like creatures. I still missed Lando, but his family had departed the space station the same day Sammy and her mom had arrived.

I hoped Sammy wouldn't choose an Inarian.

I wandered over to a large glass-fronted container built into the side wall of the emporium. Two lizard-like creatures lounged on permaplastic branches and watched me with hooded amber eyes. I glanced at the information panel and discovered that they were Fornaxian dragons.

"Stunning, aren't they?"

I looked to my left and saw that Micah Trigger, the emporium's owner, had joined me.

"Would you like to meet one?"

I eyed the creatures doubtfully. About the size of a small Earth dog, the dragons weren't remotely cute or cuddly. Sure, the green one had shiny, almost emerald scales that complimented its amber eyes, but the black one looked surly, as though I were giving offense by looking at it.

"I don't know," I said. "They don't look very friendly."

Mr. Trigger smiled. "If they wouldn't make good companions, I wouldn't have them in stock. They just need to get to know you."

Sammy joined us and gazed wide-eyed at the creatures. "What are those? I've never seen anything like them."

"Fornaxian dragons," answered Mr. Trigger. "Named after a mythological Earth creature. I was supposed to receive three, but something went wrong. When the crate was delivered to the shop, there were only these two."

"Do they fly," I asked.

Sammy looked at me like I was nuts, but Mr. Trigger smiled.

"Very perceptive, Cinnamon. Most people don't notice their wings until they unfurl them. They're very effectively camouflaged," he said. "Yes, they can fly."

"Wow," said Sammy. "Do they breathe fire too?"

Mr. Trigger laughed. "No. That would put them into an untradeable class. No fire, but they do like to hoard shiny objects. Another reason their discoverers called them dragons."

I pulled Sammy away from the dragons. They were really interesting, but Mom had made it clear that she didn't think I was ready for the responsibility of a pet. I didn't want to risk getting too attached.

"I thought you wanted to play with the puppies," I reminded Sammy. "You know, pick out your birthday present?"

Mr. Trigger brightened. "Oh? Which breed can I show you? Do you want a large dog or small?"

While Mr. Trigger gave Sammy the details of several dog breeds, I continued my circuit of the store. Along with the exotics like Inarians and Fornaxians, the emporium offered kittens, aquariums of fish from several solar systems, and more birds than I had names for.

By the time I completed my inspection, Sammy had settled

on a little black and tan ball of fluff. Mr. Trigger lifted the puppy from its cage and carried it to a meeting area—a section of the main room with waist-high walls where customers could interact with potential pets of the non-flying variety.

Sammy knelt inside the enclosure while I stood just outside, leaning on the half-wall that separated us. The puppy bounced and tumbled over her, wriggling and licking and generally expressing its joy in her attention.

"Isn't he perfect, Cinnamon?"

I had to admit, the little furball was adorable. "What kind is it?" I asked. "How big will it get?"

"Mr. Trigger said he's a sheltie. He's very smart and won't get too big for our quarters. I think I'll name him Fred."

"Fred? Really?"

Sammy nodded happily and rubbed Fred's belly while he attempted to lick every inch of her exposed skin.

I closed my eyes. Fred. Truly, Sammy had no imagination, no sense of style.

Mr. Trigger brought out several other puppies, but Sammy refused to relinquish Fred. Clearly, she had made her choice. Before we left the emporium, Sammy contacted her mom via wrist link and Mr. Trigger was authorized the hold the puppy until the adults could finalize the arrangements.

2
_____

That night at dinner I told Mom and Dad all about our adventure in the pet store. "Can you believe it?" I finished. "Out of all the amazing creatures in the emporium, Sammy chose a puppy. An Earth-normal puppy!"

I stabbed the last bite of synth-chicken and popped it in my mouth. When I finished chewing, I continued, "And guess what she named it?"

Mom and Dad exchanged amused glances before responding. "No idea," Mom said. "Don't keep us in suspense," said Dad.

I took a deep breath and announced, "She named him Fred."

Mom blinked. "Fred?"

Dad laughed. "Nothing wrong with that. Fred's a good solid name."

I threw my hands up in despair. "Yeah. Solid. Stable. _Normal_. Why couldn't she give it a more adventurous name?"

"What would you name a dog?" Mom asked.

I considered the question, but before I could answer, Dad's wrist link flashed red.

"Sorry, Maria," he said before Mom could object to links at the table. "This is code red, I have to take it."

Mom nodded. "We were finished anyway. Cinnamon, help me clear the table, please."

Sammy and Fred were relegated to the back of my mind as I lingered in the eating nook trying to accidentally overhear Dad's conversation. Mom was wise to my tricks though. "Cinnamon, on task, please."

"Yes, ma'am," I answered, stifling both a sigh *and* an eye-roll.

Mom and I were just finishing up when Dad joined us in the kitchen. He kissed Mom's cheek and ruffled my short dark hair. "I've got to go to the market sector," he said, slipping into his blue and silver USL uniform jacket. "There's been a rash of thefts. Mostly inexpensive jewelry and small metallic objects, but a few valuable items are missing as well. I want to examine the affected shops as quickly as possible."

Mom nodded, but I spoke up. "Can I come with you?"

"I don't know, Sugar Cookie," he said, a slight frown creasing his brow. "This is official business; an active crime scene."

"I promise I'll stay out of the way," I said quickly. "I won't be any bother." I crossed my fingers behind my back and held my breath while he considered.

Dad glanced at Mom. "What do you think, Maria?"

"Up to you, Li. The chances of you actually encountering the thief are negligible, so she'll be in no danger. The only question is whether or not she'll interfere with your work."

"I won't," I said, trying to keep my voice from rising to a shrill squeal.

Mom gave me her famous remain-quiet-if-you-know-what's-good-for-you glare, and I zipped my lips.

Dad eyed me thoughtfully. After what felt like an eternity while I stood still (despite nerves that made me want to bounce off the walls), kept my mouth shut (SO hard when I wanted to beg for this opportunity to learn about real detective work), and tried to look mature and responsible (I was twelve years old, after all!), Dad nodded. "All right, Cinnamon. You may come. But," he pointed a finger at me and gave me his best commanding officer expression, "you will obey my every command immediately and without question. Is that understood?"

"Sir! Yes, sir," I responded with a crisp salute.

"Very well. Follow me, Detective-in-training Chou."

I stifled a squeal, beamed at Mom, and followed Dad into the corridor.

Space station corridors can be very confusing. A person new to the station often thinks they all look alike, but they're wrong. You just have to get used to the subtle clues. Since I've grown up on Space Station Zeta, I'm never lost. I can tell purple sector from blue without even having to resort to the colored chips embedded in the corridor walls and floors. I can tell the sectors by their odors.

Green sector houses hydroponics and smells of nutrients, water and growing plants. Red sector is mechanical engineering. If you think nanobots and computer circuitry don't have distinct odors, then you've never lived on a space station. Blue sector is administration, which translates to military since Space Station Zeta is a Universal Star League station. As such the station is under the command and protection of the USL Fleet. Both of my parents are USL officers, so blue sector smells of peace, security, and home.

Not that we lived in blue sector. All living quarters were in the central core—yellow sector. Yellow was further divided into crew and civilian quarters, and then by individual or family, but beyond that our station had no class boundaries. At least not where living quarters were concerned.

And then there's white sector. Medics and remedies; antiseptics and bile; with a stiff overlay of fear. I hated even walking past white sector.

But now I followed Dad to purple sector, the market district. Purple always smells of hot oil, spices, and too many humans and aliens packed into too little space—even now, when many of Space Station Zeta's inhabitants had returned to their quarters for the dinner hour.

I practiced my stealth mode as I followed Dad from shop to shop, trying to stay close, be unobtrusive, and soak up as much of Dad's investigative technique as possible. We examined display cases, noted unusual patterns of destruction, and searched for entry and exit points.

All of the affected shops were empty at the time of the theft, the owners having locked up for the three-hour break between afternoon and evening commerce that most of the market sector observed. I stepped carefully across what looked like an old Earth tree branch that had been knocked to the floor by the thief and stopped beside Dad.

"And you're sure you locked the doors when you left?" Dad asked the proprietor.

"Yes, sir. I ran through my usual closing routine. The doors were locked, and as you can see we don't have any windows other than the front display, and it's in tact."

Dad nodded and I followed his gaze as he studied the small shop. Bits of jewelry littered the terra cotta colored permaplastic floor along with the decorative branch. The enclosed glass cases were undisturbed, though items had been swept from their tops. A manikin standing sentinel near the door was missing its wig (which rested on the floor at its feet like a small, furry pet), but its clothing still hung in meticulously arranged folds.

When Dad turned his attention to the ceiling, I saw his eyes narrow. That's when I noticed the air vent. The screen covering dangled from the duct at a precarious angle.

"How long has that vent cover been damaged?" Dad asked

the owner, pointing to the eighteen-inch opening near the ceiling.

"What? We don't have..." his words sputtered to a halt as he saw the damaged vent. Frowning, he said, "I'm sure that was fine when I left the shop."

"Aikens," Dad called, and a young man dressed in USL blue and silver and wearing a security badge snapped to attention. "Yes, sir?" he said.

"Make a quick tour of the other affected shops. Notice if others have damaged air vents," he said, pointing upward.

"Right away, sir!" Aikens turned and strode from the shop.

The owner watched Aikens' departure and then turned to Dad. "Surely you don't think the thief used the vent," he said. "It's too small. Why, even your daughter would be too big for such an opening, plus, the culprit would need to fly to leave by the same opening."

I didn't hear Dad's reply; I'd stopped listening. I stared at the gaping vent and imagined a pair of amber eyes staring back at me. Mr. Trigger's words from earlier in the day echoed in my memory, *Fornaxian dragons ... I was supposed to receive three, but something went wrong. When the crate was delivered to the shop, there were only these two.*

I tugged on Dad's jacket sleeve.

"Not now, Cinnamon," he said as Aikens stopped in front of him.

"But Dad..." He silenced me with hand movement.

"Report, Aikens."

Aikens straightened and said, "Sir, each shop has a damaged air vent. All appear to have been pushed outward from inside the vent."

Dad nodded, gazing thoughtfully at the vent. I tugged on his sleeve again.

"What part of 'not now' do you not understand, Detective-in-training Chou?"

I squared my shoulders and met his gaze boldly. "Sir, I have pertinent information to report."

Dad lifted an eyebrow, but said, "Very well. Report, Chou."

"Sir, when Sammy and I visited Trigger's Exotic Creature Emporium, Mr. Trigger mentioned a discrepancy in his inventory." I paused and Dad nodded for me to continue. "He had expected three Fornaxian dragons, but only two were delivered."

"I see, and do these dragons fly and breathe fire?"

"No sir, they do not breathe fire," I said, then hurried to add, "but they do fly and Mr. Trigger reports that they like to hoard shiny objects." That's when my excitement got the better of me and I dropped my detective-in-training act. "Isn't everything that's missing shiny? And a good-sized flying lizard-y creature would be able to come and go through the vents! I'm right, aren't I, Dad? Someone on the loading dock lost one of the dragons and it escaped into the air vents."

Dad nodded. "That's a plausible theory, Cinnamon. Thank you for the information. We'll investigate the possibility, but right now, it's time for you to go home. Aikens!"

My shoulders dropped. "You mean I don't get to see this through to the end?"

Dad crouched down to my eye level. "This isn't a punishment, Sugar Cookie. I think you've probably just solved the mystery, but it's getting late and I'm going to be moving all over the station following this lead. You need your sleep. I'll let you know what happens in the morning." He straightened, tousled my hair, and turned to Aikens. "Please escort my daughter back to our quarters, then report to me in the cargo bay."

Aikens smiled at me. "It will be my pleasure, sir."

3

The next morning at breakfast, Dad told Mom all about how I'd cracked the case for him. Mom listened thoughtfully and when Dad finished his report, smiled.

"Well done, Cinnamon. I'm very proud of you and I'm sure Dad is as well."

I swallowed a mouthful of protein-rich, calcium-enhanced syntho-juice, wiped my mouth on a recycled napkin and said, "Thanks, Mom. Dad, did they catch the dragon yet?"

"No, but we found its hoard by sending the cleaning robot through the ducts and caught a glimpse of the red devil. Mr. Trigger has arranged a nice display of glittering jewelry to tempt it into an enclosure. All the merchants donated their shiniest pieces to the trap—Mr. Trigger assured them that nothing would be damaged—and they've removed anything else that might interest a dragon from their shelves for the day. We expect to have the perp in custody by evening."

I giggled. "I don't envy the kid who ends up with that creature for a pet."

Dad raised an eyebrow. "Truly? Mr. Trigger said he'd be delighted to place the unexpected dragon in your custody," he said, "as long as you promise to take good care of it and teach it not to steal."

My eyes widened and I stared at Dad, then Mom, then back to Dad. "Really? You'd let me have a Fornaxian dragon?"

Mom smiled. "I think you've proven yourself responsible enough for a pet."

"You don't have to accept," Dad said. "But if you want this little red devil, it's yours."

I thought of the other two dragons, the gleaming scales of the emerald one and the surly glare of the black one. What would the red one be like? Obviously intelligent. Definitely exotic. Just the kind of pet I'd always dreamed of.

No solid, stable, *normal* pet for me. No sir. Cinnamon Chou, space station detective, needed a pet with spunk and imagination. Now I just needed to find a suitably adventurous name for dragon who was about to become a reformed thief!

COPYRIGHT

THE CASE OF THE RECREATIONAL THIEF

1

$\mathcal{T}$he door to my bedroom irised open with a nearly inaudible *whoosh*, and I stepped inside clutching Dad's gift to my chest. I couldn't believe my luck! My very first grown-up, never-owned-by-anyone-else tablet, complete with security features encoded to my thumbprint and DNA.

Not even Mom or Dad would be able to access this tablet without my permission. How cool was that?

I hopped up onto my built-in bunk, settled the tablet on my knees, opened my very first folder, and titled it: *The Case Files of Cinnamon Chou, Space Station Detective.*

A happy sigh escaped my lips. I might still be a kid, but I had big dreams. I was going to be a Universal Star League detective, just like my dad. By the time I was old enough to attend the USL Academy, I intended to have a sizable number of cases documented in my files.

That's how I'd gotten this tablet. I'd prepared my case, presented my argument (referencing my Academy aspirations), and Mom and Dad had agreed to my request.

"All right, Sugar Cookie," Dad said—he was the only living being (human *or* alien) who was allowed to refer to me as the overly sweet pastry responsible for my name. The story goes that the first instant he saw me, he told my mother that my combination of her ebony complexion and his gold-toned coloration reminded him of an old-fashioned cinnamon sugar cookie.

Parents.

What can you do with them?

Anyway, Dad said, "All right, Sugar Cookie. You've made your case. We'll get you a secure tablet...on one condition."

I held my breath to keep from screaming in delight and waited for him to elaborate.

He glanced at Mom, received a minuscule nod, and said, "Like any commanding officer, your mother and I reserve the right to review your files." He lifted an eyebrow and waited for my response.

I considered for a mere heartbeat before nodding. "Sir, yes sir," I said, giving him a crisp USL salute. "As a junior detective under your command, my files will be open for your inspection." I paused, licked my lips, and countered. "But only when requested in advance and reviewed in my presence."

Mom and Dad exchanged glances. Mom, as senior USL officer present, nodded. "That is acceptable, Junior Detective Chou. You will have your tablet within the week. Dismissed."

I pumped my fist, squealed and ran to hug them. First Dad, then Mom; then, in an excess of exuberance, both at once. "Thank you! This is going to be so awesome!"

Dad tousled my hair, and Mom grinned. "You did a great job building your case, Cinnamon. We can't wait to see the case files you write."

Secure in my bedroom, I created my first file: *The Case of the Missing Inarian*.

A broad beam of sadness swept through my heart and tears misted my vision. That had been my best friend Lando Maxon's last day on Space Station Zeta, and I still missed him terribly. Writing up that case would be a bittersweet reminder of a great friend.

I glanced across the room to the habitat Dad and I had built for my very first pet, a handsome red Fornaxian dragon I'd named Raphael. Rafe, a reformed thief, would be the focus of my second file: *The Case of the Glittering Hoard.*

When I finished transferring my hand written case notes to my new tablet, I pulled on the special sheath glove Dad had designed for me, opened Rafe's habitat, and invited him onto my forearm. The glove protected my skin (and my tunic) from Rafe's claws. Dad said it served a similar purpose to protective gear used by his ancient ancestors, the eagle hunters of a place on Earth known as Mongolia.

Rafe eyed my extended arm for a moment before deciding to take me up on the invitation to leave his habitat. He unfurled his ruby-red wings and flew from one of his perches to my arm. I managed to take his weight without bobbling; I was definitely getting stronger. Rafe was easily the size of a small Earth dog, one of those described as "lap dogs." He was red scaled, with a barbed tail that was nearly as long as his body.

When he first came to me, his expression was haughty and aloof, like he was doing me a favor by making eye contact. Now that we'd been together for a few months he actually seemed to like me, even chirping and purring and nuzzling my cheek when he perched on my arm or shoulder.

Of course, his good mood was probably ninety-percent due to the amazing habitat Dad had created. Rafe's "cage" easily took up half of my bedroom. It rose from floor to ceiling, included multiple permaplastic perches that reminded me of tree limbs, and had a small pond on the floor for both drinking and bathing.

I was responsible for keeping his habitat clean, and believe me, it was a chore—especially cleaning that pond. But I was lucky... Fornaxian dragons are very clean animals. Rafe used one specific corner of his habitat as a toilet, and as long as I kept that area well supplied with faux-cedar chips, scooping out the refuse was a breeze.

Stepping out of the habitat with Rafe on my arm, I strode from my bedroom to our living room.

"I'm taking Rafe to the recreation area," I called to my parents. "We'll be back before dinner."

"Have fun," Mom said, looking up from the novel she was reading on her tablet.

"Don't forget to work on his training exercises," Dad said.

I grinned and palmed the door open. "Don't worry. Rafe and I are getting really good at working together. We're a good team!"

2

_____

he recreation area was actually a large park at the center of yellow sector. All living quarters were located at the central core of Space Station Zeta and were designated as yellow sector. The area was divided into crew and civilian quarters, and then by individual or family units, but beyond that our station had no class distinctions. At least not where living quarters were concerned.

The ground in the recreation area was artificial turf. That springy green stuff that's supposed to mimic old Earth grass. Since I've never experienced the original plant life, I can't say how closely the turf matched its model, but it worked for me. We had game fields (soccer, baseball, and galactic jumpball), trees (like the ever present Andolian fern trees), and lots of open space where kids like me could run and jump and play made-up games.

Rafe and I headed straight for the middle of the open space. I gave him the "fly free" sign, and he launched from my arm, soaring into the high-ceilinged "sky." He circled the field three times before heading over to the Andolian ferns and landing on a sturdy branch. Once stationary, he began grooming himself, flicking his long tongue over every scale on his body. I was still amazed that he could actually groom the top of his head and the back of his neck... talk about limber. When he finished, his scales gleamed like faceted gems in the clear, simulated sunlight.

Rabbie, a boy in my educational unit, jogged up to me.

"Hey, Cinnamon, wanna play jumpball?" he asked. "Or are you too busy admiring your dragon?"

I glanced sideways at him. "Who else is playing?"

He nodded toward a knot of kids a few yards away. "We've got Ginger and Liu and Aaron and Jase. Sammy said she'd come back as soon as she took Fred home."

Before I could stop myself, I rolled my eyes, exasperated by the name my best friend on the whole station had given her Earth-normal puppy.

"What?" asked Rabbie.

"Fred," I said. "Have you ever heard a stupider name for a puppy?"

He glanced down and shrugged. "I dunno. He's her dog. She can call him what she wants."

"Yeah. I know. But seriously... Fred? Surely Sammy could've come up with something a little more interesting."

"It's just a name, *Cinnamon*," he said, giving my name just a little too much emphasis.

We joined the other kids and played a quick game of jump-ball, while Rafe circled the field chittering and screaming his encouragement.

At least *I* knew it was encouragement.

The other kids seemed to find a dragon flying over their heads worrisome. Even though Sammy hadn't returned, I called Rafe back to my wrist when the first game ended and headed home.

"See you tomorrow," I yelled to my friends, who waved back, looking just a bit too relieved at our departure.

But the next day, my world fell apart.

3

_____

*B*efore class even started Sammy stormed up to me, fists on hips and eyes sparkling with anger. "Why do you have to be so mean about Fred?" she asked.

I'd never seen her so angry, and I didn't have a clue what she was talking about. I mean, aside from his ridiculous name, Fred was an adorable little black and tan ball of fluff. Who could be mean to a little guy whose only aim in life was to wriggle and lick you and beg for belly rubs?

"I'm not mean to Fred," I said, feeling hurt and confused. "I think Fred is sweet."

"Not *to* Fred," she said, exasperation clear in her voice, "*about* him. His name."

She paused, glaring at me. Probably waiting for me to defend myself. I decided silence was my best defense.

"Rabbie told me what you said," she clarified. Then, with a smug little grin, added, "He also said he thought it was pretty rich for someone named *Cinnamon*, whose dad calls her *Sugar Cookie*, to be making fun of anyone else's name."

I glanced around, found Rabbie, and stabbed him with a glare.

Turning my attention back to Sammy, I said, in my best calm-and-collected voice, "Look, he's your puppy, but even you have to admit that Fred is a goofy name for a dog."

Sammy's eyes narrowed and she turned redder than I'd ever imagined my pale-skinned, blonde friend could manage. "You're a fine one to talk. You named that stupid dragon Ralph."

My temper flared. "Did not! His name is Rafe, and it's short for Raphael. Which you know perfectly well."

"Ralph!" she taunted. "And everyone knows..." she paused for dramatic effect, "...Ralph is a thief!"

I'd never wanted to punch anyone in the face as much as I did right then. My thoughts smoldered and my fists clenched, but I turned around and walked away. Mom and Dad would be proud... but that didn't make me feel any better.

My best friend in the whole space station had just betrayed me.

I hated her!

The rest of the day, we stayed as far away from each other as possible. Our teacher, Mrs. Sheffield, looked at us with bemused concern, but didn't insist on us working together. Which was unusual. Normally, Sammy and I were inseparable.

But not today. Today, we were mortal enemies.

After school, I stormed into my bedroom, released Rafe from his habitat, and plopped onto my back on my bed. Rafe circled the room a couple of times before landing on the bed beside me. Crooning, he stretched out between my arm and my side and rested his head on my shoulder.

Ruby red love with gleaming amber eyes.

His crooning changed to a purr... which soothed my frazzled nerves.

I stroked his long, lean body, feeling content for the first time since my fight with Sammy.

"What do I need her for when I've got you?" I smiled, a little sadly, and closed my eyes. "You're the only friend I need."

I knew in my heart that wasn't true, but saying it made me feel better.

4

The next day at school, things got even worse!

Groups of chattering kids suddenly fell silent when I approached, their gazes following me as I walked from room to room.

What? I wanted to yell. What have I done now?

But I didn't.

By lunchtime, I'd reached my limit. I marched over to the table where Rabbie and Ginger and Liu were sitting with Sammy. "What's going on?" I demanded. "Why is everyone treating me like I have an infectious disease?"

Rabbie glanced around the table for support, then stood and faced me. "Haven't you heard? Stuff has been going missing from the recreation area."

I narrowed my eyes, my gaze flitting from him to the others sitting at the table and back again. "What kind of stuff?"

Sammy caught my gaze and held it. "Shiny stuff," she said meaningfully.

"And you think..." I stopped. I didn't want to say it out loud.

Sammy nodded. "Ralph. Everyone knows he was caught red-pawed stealing shiny jewelry in the purple sector."

"He didn't do it," I cried. "I mean, yes, he was guilty of the market sector robberies, but that was before I adopted him. He's reformed now. He hasn't stolen anything since he came to live with us."

"That you know of," Rabbie said, so smugly that I wanted to punch him.

Wow. That was the second time in two days I'd felt like punching one of my friends!

I controlled my anger... and my worry... and turned around and left.

Did I even have any friends anymore?

Feeling more than a little nauseous, I excused myself for the rest of the day and ran home. As it was the middle of the day and both my parents were on duty, Rafe was my only confidant. I released him from his habitat and he flew beside me as I paced through the rooms of our living quarters.

"Think, Cinnamon," I told myself. "Think. You know Rafe's not guilty. How are you going to prove it?"

I raced to my room, my dragon shadowing my movements, and grabbed my new tablet. The answer was obvious. I had to solve the case! Opening a new file, I titled it *The Case of the Recreational Thief* and began to type out my thoughts.

I was a detective. The daughter of an excellent detective. I could do this.

But first, I needed to gather evidence. I needed to visit the scene of the crime.

5

———

*T*he recreational area was deserted in the middle of the day. All the school age kids were busy with lessons and the littles were undoubtedly napping. Adults were either on duty, at their jobs, or sleeping in preparation for their next shift. Rafe and I had the place to ourselves.

I placed my new tablet carefully on a picnic table and plopped onto the bench. Scanning the area, I allowed my thoughts to simmer.

I doubted the thief was human... or one of the sapient alien species who inhabited Space Station Zeta. The missing items weren't valuable enough for even a child to steal.

But they were all shiny... and small. Things that caught and refracted the light, but were small enough for a Fornaxian dragon to carry away.

Not that he did. Because he didn't.

A stylus. A faceted glass marble. A chocolate bar with a shiny wrapper.

Things of too little value to be of concern to my dad's security force. I was the only detective interested enough to take on the case... and my motivation wasn't the recovery of stolen property, it was clearing my dragon's good name.

Rafe flew around the recreation area, circling the open space and flitting from tree to tree in the forested part, while I puzzled over the culprit's identity.

If it wasn't one of the human or alien *people*, then it must be a creature. Since the space station didn't have wild animals like the squirrels and chipmunks or even rats of Earth, any critter living in the park would have to be feral. A pet that had gotten loose, very likely when its owners cycled off station.

That could've easily happened to my friend Lando's Inarian. The small, hamster-like creature had escaped from its cage the morning Lando and his family were leaving the station. If I hadn't helped him find the little furball, Dumpling could've been left behind. But I couldn't see an Inarian surviving in the wild, let alone stealing non-food objects.

I reviewed a mental list of station pets.

Dogs; not likely.

Cats; probably smart enough, but with no motive that I could see.

Fish; uhm... no.

Dragons; definitely capable and prone to hoarding shiny objects, but since the only ones on station were my Rafe and the two that remained in *Trigger's Exotic Creature Emporium*, I ruled them out.

Birds.

I frowned, glancing at the sky. Birds had a lot in common with my dragon. They could fly. Some species were very smart; some could even talk. They were inquisitive, and were perfectly capable of picking up a small, shiny object if it caught their interest. And they were frequently brought aboard as pets.

I cocked my head and studied the Andolian fern tree forest. Could the thief be living wild in those trees?

Whistling for Rafe, I designed a two-fold trap. I didn't know how much Standard Rafe understood, but I knew he was smart, and I knew he understood more of what I told him than my parents would believe. When he landed on the picnic table beside my tablet, I explained our dilemma.

"So," I finished, "I want you to fly through the forest and look for a nest, one with a hoard of shiny objects. Stuff you might like if I didn't give you lots of nice things for your very own."

Rafe cocked his head and closed his amber eyes very slowly. When he opened them again, he bounced his head once before leaping into flight.

Great. Trap one was in motion.

Digging around in the pocket of my tunic, I pulled out an inexpensive bracelet that sparkled in the sunlight and a small mirror with a gilt handle. I ran to a picnic table well away from the one where my tablet rested and placed the mirror on it in full sight. The bracelet ended up in the middle of the jumpball field where it sparkled nicely.

Returning to the picnic table I'd claimed as my base of operations, I glanced back and forth from the mirror to the bracelet. Trap two was baited and ready.

I soon wished I'd just put out one shiny object. My eyes got tired of shifting from one site to the other. If I wasn't careful, I'd have nothing but a nasty headache to show for my efforts.

Just then a scream sounded from the trees. A Fornaxian dragon scream.

I jumped to my feet and was about to run to the forest when two creatures burst from the greenery; a good-sized bird with glossy purple-black feathers and a bright yellow-orange patch near its head was being chased through the air by my ruby red dragon!

"Help," the bird screamed. "Help me!"

6

_____

$\mathcal{D}$ ad and Mr. Trigger came to the rescue. The *Creature Emporium* owner brought a large cage and, with a little help from Rafe, managed to capture the unhappy bird.

The cage represented safety to the bird who'd most likely been hand raised, and being chased by a ruby red dragon provided the terror that made the safety of the cage seem very appealing.

When Rafe landed on my arm, I transferred him to my shoulder, where he crooned happily and nuzzled my neck.

"It's a myna," Mr. Trigger explained. "I don't sell them, so this one must have been brought aboard as a pet."

"Well," said Dad, "since no one has reported a missing bird, his owners must have lost him when cycling off station."

Mr. Trigger nodded. "Very likely." He turned to me. "You say you heard him speak, Cinnamon?"

I grinned. "Yep. When Rafe chased him out of the trees he was screaming, 'Help me!'"

"Good to know," Mr. Trigger said. "That'll make him easier to place with a new family. Why was Rafe chasing him?"

I stroked my dragon's scales. "I asked him to find a nest with shiny things in it," I explained. "He probably found this bird examining its hoard and brought him to me."

Dad looked skeptical. "Don't you think you're giving Rafe a little too much credit, Sugar Cookie?"

I frowned. I really needed to talk to Dad about calling me that in public, but Rafe chirped indignantly at the slight, so I concentrated on him.

"He's smarter than you give him credit for, Dad. I bet he could take us to that nest right now, if I asked."

Rafe chirped his agreement.

Dad swept an arm toward the forest. "Let's see if he can do it."

After nuzzling my neck one more time, Rafe leapt into flight. Dad and Mr. Trigger and I followed. Rafe landed about fifteen feet up in a fern tree beside a nest of twigs and leaves. He cocked his head at us and then kicked the nest to the ground.

Shiny objects rained down on us along with the remains of the nest.

"Well," said Dad, raking through the debris with gloved fingers, "I guess that answers both questions; Rafe found the thief, and he's smarter than I thought." He turned a brilliant smile on me. "He definitely understood you, Sugar Cookie."

7

It didn't take long for the story of Rafe's apprehension of the recreational thief to filter through yellow sector. My ruby red dragon was a hero, his earlier thievery forgiven, if not forgotten.

That very afternoon Rafe and I ran into Sammy and Fred in the park's open space. After an uncomfortable instant we both said, "I'm sorry," at the same time.

Laughing, I held out my hand.

Sammy accepted it and we shook.

"I'm sorry I accused Rafe of stealing those things," she said.

I nodded. "And I'm sorry for making fun of Fred's name." I knelt down and the puppy wriggled over to me, turning belly up so I could rub his soft underside. Which I did. Happily.

Glancing up at Sammy, I said, "He's the cutest puppy on the station, and if you say his name is Fred, then that's fine by me. Fred's a good solid name for an adorable furball."

Sammy grinned and pointed at Rafe, who was circling the open space and showing off his rolls and flips. "Rafe is amazing," she said. "I only called him Ralph because I was mad at you. I know his name is Raphael, and Rafe is a great nickname."

Standing, I met her gaze. "Friends?"

She nodded. "Always."

We hugged each other while Rafe chittered happily and Fred wriggled in delight.

Pets (even highly intelligent Fornaxian dragons) are great, but best friends are better!

COPYRIGHT

THE JOURNAL

CHAPTER ONE

*a*rtie Woodward-Kendrick pulled down the collapsible staircase to the attic in her childhood home. She'd always hated the attic, had found any and every excuse to avoid going up there. But then, Artie's childhood had been filled with terrors.

Literally.

Creatures no one else could see.

Creatures that fed from the life energy of the people around her. She'd learned to hide from their sight, had learned to keep herself safe. But until she met her husband when they were both teens, she'd had no idea that it was possible to fight them. Her life had changed irrevocably when she met Jed Kendrick, and she'd never been happier.

Time to face yet another of her childhood fears.

Wiping sweaty palms on her well-worn jeans, Artie pushed up the sleeves of her red flannel shirt, grasped the rails of the collapsible stairs and climbed into the dim and dusty attic. She thought she heard something scurry away as she landed on the wooden floorboards, leaving dusty imprints of her sneakers with every step, but her heart was pounding so hard she couldn't be sure.

Where was Jed? He'd agreed to help her with this.

Her parents were selling the house and moving into a condominium and while they sorted and packed the contents of the main floors, she'd been given the task of inspecting the attic and determining what was worth keeping and what should simply be lobbed into the trash bin. She'd wanted to refuse, but her parents were so proud of what they saw as her recovery from her childhood instability ... well, she didn't want to disappoint them. And she *was* strong now. But she was so much stronger with Jed by her side.

She found the slender pull chain that controlled the single light bulb attached to one of the rafters and yanked it on. Light flooded the center of the room, but left the edges and the spaces behind boxes and old wardrobes in shadow. She shivered, but forced herself to walk deeper into the room.

It's just old stuff, she told herself sternly. *There's nothing here that can harm me. It's only creepy because there's not enough light and everything is covered in dust and cobwebs. There's nothing dangerous living in my parents' attic.*

She'd reached the grimy, round window at the far end of the room when a noise on the staircase started her heart pounding again. Turning to face the hole in the floor, she saw a dark head appear. Her racing heartbeat and jittery stomach urged her to scream, but she stifled the impulse. A moment later, she smiled as the man of her dreams stepped into the attic's dim light.

"Hey, sweetheart," Jed said in a cheerful voice as he surveyed the boxes and dilapidated furniture. "Sorry I'm late. How do you want to tackle this?"

Artie released the breath she hadn't realized she'd been holding and gestured around the room. "Pick a box, any box, and evaluate the contents. Let's make three piles: one to keep, one to trash, and one to donate."

"Sounds like a plan," he said, clapping his hands. "Let's get started."

Artie had moved three boxes to the trash heap and one box of out-of-fashion, but serviceable clothes to the donation pile, when Jed gave a low whistle.

"Come take a look at this, Artie."

He stood before an ancient piece of furniture, a secretary her mother would call it. The slanted lid opened to become a flat writing surface and the back portion was filled with little drawers and cubbies for holding who knew what.

"Look what I found," Jed said, his voice loud in the still room. "A kind of secret compartment."

She walked over to stand beside him. What looked like a carved, columnar divider between two of the cubbies was actually a hidden vertical drawer. Jed had accidentally loosened it, and taking a chance, had pulled. It slid out revealing a book with a cracked leather binding and yellowing pages.

But even more unexpected than its hiding place was the book itself. The volume glowed to Artie and Jed's special sight. For Artie Woodward and Jed Kendrick weren't normal humans. They were *Sidhe Seers*. Both were descendants of an ancient Irish clan which had been given the ability to see the Sidhe, the ancient Celtic name for what the mundane world called fairies.

Jed could trace his lineage directly to the ancient O'Connors, but Artie had no idea where her connection originated. She only knew that she could see what she'd always termed *Terrors*, but now knew were a particular race of Fae.

"What do you think it is?" she asked, her earlier nervousness slamming back into action. "Do you think it's safe to touch?"

Jed shrugged. "Only one way to find out," and he pulled the

book from its hiding space, opened the cover, and began to read aloud.

January 30, 1919

    My name is Maeve O'Connor Woodward and this is my journal.

    I'm a newly married woman and a Sidhe Seer. My husband, Michael Woodward, is an English groom. He accompanied his lord from his home in Somerset to the lord's newly purchased manor in the Dublin countryside last year. Michael and I met when he was sent to my family's farm to buy hay and oats for the lord's stables.

    I fell in love with him at first sight. Tall and well-built, with golden hair and gray-blue eyes, so unlike the local lads. I longed to run my fingers through that hair, thick and wavy, it was, and the strands that had come loose from the black ribbon with which he'd tied it back enticed me. His hair didn't spring into unruly curls like my own auburn locks, and I wondered what it would feel like between my fingers. Smooth as silk, I imagined. Not the knotted mess mine so often became.

    I'm not sure Michael even noticed me that day, but as I would soon come to know, our fates had been bound by the Sidhe, or as some have come to call them, the Fair Folk. 'Tis my belief that they're so called in order not to offend, for the Sidhe I've seen are far from fair. To be sure, ungifted mortals who've been granted a glimpse of the Sidhe are always astounded by their beauty, but that is because they see only the glamour the Sidhe choose to allow.

    I'm a Sidhe Seer, from a long line of seers. I see past their glamours to their true countenances, whether they wish to be seen or not. 'Tis a blessing and a curse. I'm not likely to fall prey to their tricks, but if they realize I see them when they believe themselves hidden ... well, 'tis a fine line I walk in order to secure the safety of me and mine.

    But I digress.

    I was telling you that this is my book. I am keeping this journal to secure a record of my gifts for future generations. If you are reading this, you are my descendent and have seen things that make you doubt your sanity. Fear not. You are a Sidhe Seer too and this diary will instruct you in the use of your gifts.

And why should you need a book of instruction, you ask? Why does your family not teach you what you need to know?

Because Michael and I have left the old country. We have travelled to the new world and moved far inland to the very roots of the Rocky Mountains. We have done this to escape the Sidhe. They have yet to come to this part of the world and our new home is free from their taint. We hope to raise our children and our children's children without their loathsome presence.

But I have no confidence that they will never find their way to this sanctuary, so I leave this record to guide those of my blood who might someday have need of its wisdom.

CHAPTER TWO

*J*ed paused in his reading and glanced at Artie. "Well, now we know where your seer blood comes from."

She nodded. "Too bad I didn't find this years ago. It would've spared me a lot of grief to know who and what I am. Do you think we should tell my folks?"

Jed frowned. "You get it from your Dad's bloodline according to Maeve's name ... has he ever shown any sign that he has *The Sight*?"

"No, and he never tried to talk to me, to tell me I wasn't alone." She shrugged. "They both acted like they thought I was nuts and carted me off to a psychiatrist before I learned to hide. I think *The Sight* skipped him."

Jed nodded. "According to Granny O'Toole, that's common." He paused, frowning at the book. "Plus, there's something weird about this book."

"Other than the fact it glows?" she asked.

He grinned. "Yeah, other than that. It's the way she assumes that if you're reading it, you have *The Sight*. I wonder...."

He wiped his dusty fingers on his jeans, grabbed Artie's hand and pulled her to the stairs. "Let's test a theory."

They clambered down the collapsible stairs and wound their way around boxes and packing supplies to the kitchen where Artie's mother, Estelle Woodward, was carefully wrapping dishes in newsprint and wedging them into a cardboard box.

"Hey, Estelle," Jed said, leaning against a counter a few feet from where his mother-in-law worked. "How's it going?"

Estelle looked up at the two young people, wiped a strand of hair out of her face with the back of her hand, and smiled. "Getting there." She leaned against the counter as well, happy to take a break from the repetitive work of reaching, wrapping, and bending. "How's the attic coming along."

"We're making progress," Artie said, finding an open bit of floor space and dropping to sit cross-legged.

"Actually," said Jed, "we just found a hidden compartment in an old secretary. This was stashed inside." He held the book out to Estelle. "Thought you might like to see it."

"How odd," she said, accepting the book and examining the cover. "A hidden compartment ... that sounds very intriguing."

The back door opened before she could say more and Richard Woodward stepped into the kitchen carrying a drill and a small blue tool box. He glanced around in surprise.

"What's this?" Richard asked. "Break time?"

"Jed and Artie discovered a secret compartment in an old piece of furniture in the attic," Estelle explained. She held up the book. "This was inside. Any idea what it is?"

Richard placed the drill and tool box on the counter and took the book from his wife. "No idea," he said, opening the cover and flipping through the pages. "Why would anyone hide a blank book?"

Jed laughed, a bit too heartily to Artie's ears, and took the book back from Richard. "It's a mystery. Probably something someone put away to give as a gift and forgot where they hid it. Interesting old secretary though. Do you want to keep it, or should I mark it for charity?"

Estelle grimaced. "Charity, definitely. If it's been tucked in the attic, we haven't needed it, and we already have too much furniture in the main house for our new condo."

"Right," said Artie, scrambling to her feet. "Well, come on, Jed. It's back to work for us."

"Thanks, kids," said Richard. "We really appreciate your help."

"I'm going to order a pizza for lunch," Estelle said. "We'll call you down when it gets here."

"Sweet!" Jed grabbed Artie's hand and gave her a quick tug. "Race you to the attic."

CHAPTER THREE

*O*nce back in the attic's dim light, Artie turned to her husband. "Well, we learned a couple of things."

Jed nodded. "Your dad's definitely not a seer."

"And Maeve had mad skills," added Artie. "I wonder how she managed to write words that only another seer can read?"

"Dunno. Maybe that'll be one of the lessons she'll cover later in the book." He opened the journal and flipped through the pages, each one crammed with small, precise penmanship. Every page was filled, even the back cover bookplate.

Artie took the book from him, walked to the end of the room and propped it against the grimy round window. "I'm anxious to learn more from my great-great-grandmother," she said, "but right now, we need to earn our pizza."

Jed moved to stand beside her. Placing an arm around her shoulders, he reached out with his free hand and stroked the journal's cover. "We're looking forward to learning what you have to teach, Maeve."

Artie rested her head on his shoulder for a moment, then drilled a finger playfully into his side. "Come on, you. There's sorting to be done!"

As they moved to tackle yet more forgotten boxes, Artie surveyed the attic and sighed with contentment. Yet another childhood fear banished. Too bad she hadn't conquered it years ago. If she'd found that book when she was young, her life might have been very different.

Her gaze fell on Jed, earnestly rifling through a box of long disused household items.

No, she wouldn't waste time worrying about what might have been. The events of her life had led her to Jed, and he was worth every awkward or unpleasant moment she'd ever endured. Knowledge was good, and she didn't doubt that they'd learn a lot from Maeve's journal, but she'd learned from experience that knowledge came when the time was right ... and this book had come to her now.

She smiled and opened another box. Now, when she and Jed could study the journal together.

The timing was perfect!

COPYRIGHT

SKYE DREAMS

1

I dreamed of him again last night. The unbelievably handsome man with long black hair and eyes as dark as a winter night. I've dreamed of him many times in the eight years since my sixteenth birthday. Always the same dream. He smiles at me and tells me I am his destiny and he is mine... and that he waits for me in sky.

Not in *the* sky, but *in sky*. I've never understood what he meant by that odd phrase. How can he wait for me in the sky? When I was younger, I wondered if I should apply to train as an astronaut, but astrophysics and the science of flight never held any appeal. Instead, I majored in history. Celtic history, to be exact, and in my studies, I found a clue to this mysterious man's comment.

What if he wasn't speaking of the atmosphere above the earth, but of the Isle of Skye? Could the man of my dreams be waiting for me on an island off the coast of Scotland?

Last night he answered some of my questions. He told me that the time is near, that his name is Angus MacDubh and he waits for me in Skye, on the Trotternish peninsula at the table of the kwa-ring. I've no clue where that is (or even *what* it is), but a little Internet research should clear up the mystery.

I don't know whether or not it's a prudent choice, but I'm going to Skye. After eight years of dreams, it's time to find out if Angus MacDubh is a real man or just a figment of my imagination. At least Skye is real. I've always wanted to travel and I can justify this trip to my family as part of my research for my doctoral thesis.

They don't know about my dream man... and I'm not about to tell them. At least, not yet.

2

I rose and dressed quickly in tan walking shorts, red T-shirt, and the sturdy hiking boots I'd broken in on hikes around my Indiana home. Ready for the day's adventure, I strode into the common room of the bed and breakfast where I had rented a room just outside the village of Staffin on Scotland's Isle of Skye.

My journey here had been a dream-come-true. I was finally traveling abroad; seeing the sights in a foreign country. And not just any country, Scotland! The place where so many of the events I'd studied had taken place.

What an adventure! I'd flown from my home in Indianapolis to New York City's bustling JFK International Airport— an adventure in itself for a midwestern girl like me!— and then boarded a flight to Glasgow. After an exhausting day of sightseeing in Scotland's most populous city, I took a train to Mallaig on the west coast of the Highlands. From there, I travelled "over the sea to Skye."

The whole time I was on that ferry, the words to the famous *Skye Boat Song* swirled through my head, commemorating Bonnie Prince Charlie's flight from the battlefield of Culloden. I was following the path of legend, and imagined myself to be Flora MacDonald spiriting the hunted prince from Scotland to my family's estates in Skye.

And then I set foot on the Isle of Skye... and felt at once that I had come home.

The village of Armadale, where the ferry docked, sat in a green, fertile valley surrounded by low hills and bordered by the sea. Though the village was quaint and lovely, it couldn't account for the emotion that welled in my soul when I stepped from the ferry onto the dock. The breeze swirled around me, cooling my face and caressing my hair, and I imagined a voice spoke to me— my dream man's voice— welcoming me home.

How odd. I'd never heard that my family was connected to Skye. If the dark-haired man hadn't begun visiting my dreams, I doubt I'd have chosen to study Celtic history. Everything I knew about Skye began and ended with a dream, and yet....

And yet I felt a connection to this place, to the very land beneath my feet.

Words whispered in my subconscious, *Don't delay. You are so close. Come to me, my heart!*

I raced to find the bus station and bought passage to the Trotternish town of Staffin, where I'd booked a room in a cozy little bed and breakfast.

"Are ye ready, then?" asked Mrs. Darrow, the B&B's owner.

I smiled and finished pulling my dark auburn hair into a messy bun atop my head where I could control it with a sun hat. "I am. I can't tell you how excited I am to see the Quirang, especially the Table."

"Well, I must say, I'd rest easier if ye'd let me call one of the local lads to guide ye on yer ramble."

Truth be told, I'd like that as well, but I shook my head. I didn't want any witnesses to what happened at the Table. If my dream man was there... well, I couldn't imagine how he could be, but just in case, I wanted privacy.

"Not to worry," I said brightly. "I have a great map and detailed instructions. Why, I even have pictures of the landmarks to guide me. I'll be fine... and besides, you know where I'm going."

"As ye wish." She sighed her concern, but gestured to the kitchen where a sturdy scrubbed oak table stood laden with food. "At least eat a hearty breakfast. Ye'll need yer energy for the climb."

While I loaded my plate with fried eggs, bacon, and a crusty oat scone, Mrs. Darrow bustled about her kitchen assembling food for my hike.

"Would ye like a thermos o' tea or coffee for the climb?" she asked as she packed a generous lunch into a brown paper bag.

"No thanks," I replied between bites of egg-soaked scone. "I think I'll stick with water. I'll fill my bottle before I go."

She continued to cluck over me and my preparations until I escaped out the door and down the narrow lane to the bus stop. The B&B was only about a mile from the trail head, but considering that the Quiraing walk was a loop of well over four miles, some of it through rough terrain, I decided to save my energy and take the bus.

A strange mixture of emotions boiled in my belly as I stared out the dusty bus window. Excitement, yes, but also a roiling coil of dread. Not quite fear, but an unease so deep I considered staying on the bus when it reached the drop off for the trail head.

If I were a superstitious woman, I'd've called that dread an omen.

Who was I kidding? I was a superstitious woman! Who but the superstitious would follow a dream all the way from Indiana to the Isle of Skye?

But my dream man had deserted me— my dreams had been innocuous since my arrival on the island— and a feeling of impending doom was strengthening with every turn of the bus's wheels.

I stared up at the high cliffs and shivered. They were simply a geological oddity, the result of a massive prehistoric landslip that had created impressive cliffs, hidden plateaus, and huge rock pinnacles. And yet, some unknown part of my mind insisted that they were more. My destiny was inextricably inter-twined with those peaks and valleys.

My destiny... or my death.

3

_____

The bus stopped at the car park that marked the start of the Quiraing walk. Summoning all my courage, I squashed the lingering unease and, concentrating on my excitement, climbed down from the bus. I settled my sun hat firmly atop my head, adjusted the straps of my backpack, and began my ascent of the Quiraing.

It was a beautiful, cloudless day. Blue sky above my head, rough dirt and rock path beneath my booted feet, the heady smell of earth and grass mixed with the salt tang of the not-too-distant sea. A steep grassy slope fell away to my right, while ancient cliffs towered above me on the left. I trudged on, glad for the hat that protected my head from the sun that baked the land.

After about a quarter of an hour, I came to my first real obstacle, a small stream running through a shallow, but rocky gorge. I scrambled down one side, hopped successfully across the water, and was scrambling back up the other side when a man's voice hailed me.

"Hello there," he said. "Need a hand?"

I glanced up from the rocky slope to see a man's hand extended in my direction. Without much thought, I accepted the offer and was boosted up the last few steps. Once on level footing, I pulled my hand back and studied my benefactor. Tall and blond, with sparkling blue eyes, the handsome stranger was dressed similarly to myself in khaki hiking shorts, cotton T-shirt, and a wide-brimmed flexible sun hat.

"Thanks," I said, reaching for the water bottle secured to the side of my pack.

"No problem. Nice to encounter a friendly face in this lonely place."

I glanced up in surprise, having just taken a sip of water. We were hardly alone. While the trail wasn't crowded, it wasn't deserted either. I could see four individuals moving along at a measured pace ahead of us, and if we stood still very long, the young couple behind me would join us.

Not sure quite how to respond, I asked, "Is this your first visit to the Quiraing?"

He grinned. "Definitely not. I've made this pilgrimage often during my life."

Pilgrimage. What an odd word choice.

I stowed my water bottle again and we continued up the trail.

"This is my first trip. It's certainly majestic."

He nodded. "That it is." We walked on a few paces before he glanced sideways at me and asked, "Do you mind company? If it's a solitary ramble you're after, I can drop back."

I smiled, but considered his question. Did I want company? Hadn't I declined Mrs. Darrow's offer to find a guide? But now that I was here, now that I was actually scrambling over this rough trail... maybe a knowledgeable companion would be nice. Especially one as personable and easy on the eyes as this man. I could always encourage him to continue alone when we reached the Table. If there seemed any need, that is.

After all, it was unlikely the man from my dreams would actually appear at the appointed place when he had no way of knowing when I would arrive.

Heck, I didn't even know when I would arrive.

"That's okay," I said before the pause became uncomfortable. "I'd like the company... if you don't mind pointing out the sights to me."

He grinned. "I'd be delighted. Always fun to see familiar sights through new eyes." He held out his hand. "I'm Eoin MacLeod, by the way."

I accepted his hand for the second time... and immediately felt my emotions spike, a heady mixture of attraction and something else. Anxiety. I released his hand as quickly as was politely possible. "Jane Allan."

We hiked on in silence, my unease growing with every step. I'd accepted his company, but I wasn't bound to the man. I could simply sit down on the trail and wait for the couple behind us to catch up.

Maybe I should do just that.

Maybe there was safety in numbers.

No. I was being ridiculous.

Eoin had done nothing but offer me his hand and his companionship. I had no reason to fear him. He was simply another hiker enjoying the same trail. And an experienced hiker at that.

But I'd given him my name.

Amazed, I realized that my increased anxiety at his touch had been a warning. My dream man had been warning me not to trust Eoin, not to give him my name. Well, if Angus wanted me to do, or not do, something, he was going to have to be a bit more explicit. Besides, how in the world could knowing my name hurt me?

And suddenly the answer burned in my mind: knowing a person's true name gives power over that person.

I had given Eoin power over me by telling him my name.

What a load of superstitious nonsense! The 'power of a name' thing was only true in fairy tales. Besides, I knew his name, too. We were on equal footing...

...but only if I knew what to do with the information, which I didn't.

I glanced at my hiking companion. A nice, normal (though provocatively handsome) man striding up the steep trail among the cliffs of the Quiraing. Nothing weird or uncanny about him. I shook my head. I was letting the legends and mysticism of my Celtic studies carry me away. Just because I was in Scotland didn't mean I'd left my twenty-first century pragmatism behind.

"Those cliffs up ahead," Eoin said, pulling me from my uncomfortable thoughts, "are known as The Prison."

I shook off my unease and answered. "I've read about those. They were called that because people thought they looked like fortress walls."

"Ah, you've done your homework. Good on you."

As I studied the formidable high cliffs, a question floated to the surface of my mind. What if they were called The Prison, because someone was imprisoned there?

Nonsense. If I could hike this loop, so could anyone else.

Not if they were cursed, came an imagined reply.

I shivered despite the sun's baking heat.

The trail narrowed and Eoin took the lead, striding a few paces ahead of me.

"When we round this next bend, you'll see some rather spectacular rock pinnacles," Eoin said over his shoulder. "The tallest is known as The Needle." I nodded, though he couldn't see me. I'd read about that on the Internet as well.

We hiked on for another hour, Eoin pointing out the occasional landmark as we scrambled over scree slopes, climbed stiles, and ducked under rock outcroppings. Once we came to a fork in the path marked with a cairn of stones. Eoin took the left-hand fork without hesitation, and I followed, pleased not to have to dig out my notes to refresh my memory.

We kept the main wall of cliffs on our left until we reached the cliff top, where the trail hugged the edge. The sheer drop was terrifying, but the view was amazing. Eoin pointed out the village of Staffin to the east, along with the islands of Raasay and Rona, and further across the water, the hills of Torridon on the mainland.

I felt like I could see forever... and my spirits soared.

When I'd soaked up the view, we continued on, moving away from the cliff edge and onto a worn path that soon became a series of turf steps.

Finally, we reached the summit... and my destination.

"Well," said Eoin, "we did it. This is the summit. Five hundred and forty meters, nearly eighteen hundred feet by your reckoning." He glanced at me and smiled. "You are American, aren't you? Your accent gave you away."

I returned his smile, warily. Now that we were here, my emotions were in turmoil. Intense excitement filtered by extreme anxiety made it hard for me to form a coherent thought.

"Yes," I managed to say. "I'm from Indiana, in the heartland of the USA." I walked to the cliff edge and stared down at a flat, grassy plateau surrounded by cliff walls and massive rock formations. "That's the Table, isn't it?"

Eoin joined me at the edge, and a frisson of fear zinged along my spine. "Yes. A rather austere and lonely place."

I stepped away from him, smiled, and held out my hand.

"Well, I don't want to keep you. It's been a pleasure hiking with you, Eoin."

He glanced from my outstretched hand to my face, a little frown marring his countenance. He could hardly have missed my rather pointed dismissal. The briefest moment passed before he took my hand and pulled me close. "I'm in no hurry. I think I'll take my lunch on the Table. Appropriate, don't you think?"

He was too close. But he wasn't close enough! My emotions warred. He frightened me, here in this lonely, windswept place. But the pull of desire made me long to give in to his embrace, to raise my face to his and discover his taste in a kiss so passionate we might both burst into flames.

What was I thinking?

Where were the other hikers?

I glanced around, but no one was in sight. It was as if he and I were the only people left on the planet. I tried to step back, to pull my hand free of his, but it was like moving through molasses. My movements gained me nothing.

He laughed and released me, but I remained wrapped in a web of his power.

My instincts, my unease, had been correct. This was no ordinary hiker. Whatever he was, Eoin MacLeod was not a normal man.

I tried to speak. My jaw locked; no words came out.

"Tell me the truth, Jane. Why did you come to the Table?"

He released my jaw muscles, and I said, "I'm a scholar of Celtic history. I came to see the sights. I came to see the Table."

He scowled. "Then let's see it."

He waved his hands and a whirlwind formed. The air around me screamed and bits of sandy rock stung the bare skin of my arms and legs. My hat was torn from my head and my feet lost contact with the earth.

Be calm, said a voice in my mind. My dream man's voice. Angus' voice. *He canna harm ye if ye dinna give in to him.*

I held onto that promise, though I was certain my skin was being flailed from my body. After what felt like an eternity, the winds calmed and I found myself standing in the center of a large, grassy meadow surrounded by austere cliffs and majestic rock formations.

4

I was not alone. Two men stood a few feet away. One the epitome of the modern world, blond, blue-eyed, and dressed for a morning's hike; the other from a far distant time, long dark hair clubbed at the base of his neck, and clad in a linen shirt and blue and green plaid kilt.

Eoin MacLeod and Angus MacDubh.

It seemed the man of my dreams did exist. And, from the way they glared at each other, that he and my hiking companion were acquainted.

"Ye've no right to interfere," Angus said.

"And you've no way to stop me," Eoin replied.

My shaking legs betrayed me and I collapsed onto the grass of the Table. At least Eoin had spared me the treacherous climb down from the summit, though I doubted the scramble would have been as harrowing as the whirlwind he had called. Why was I here? Who were these men? What power did Eoin possess to be able to call the wind? For that matter, what power gave Angus the ability to invade my dreams?

And what did either of them want from me?

"Leave the lass out of this," Angus said, his voice quiet, but menacing.

Eoin's eye's flashed. "I tried to! Did I not send her forward in time? Did I not cause her soul to be reborn in a foreign land, far from the soil of Skye?"

He turned from Angus, strode a few steps closer to me, then whirled and returned to my dream man. "It was *you* who called her back; *you* who are the reason she is here... and in peril."

Peril? Anxiety clawed at the edges of my mind; I fought to calm it. What peril was I in other than feeling a bit topsy-turvy from Eoin's whirlwind?

"So I did," Angus retorted. "She is my life, my own... my destiny. Once she was reborn into this world, I could not but call her. And ye have no right to keep her from me."

"I can't let her join you," Eoin said. "You know I can't."

"Aye, I know." Angus sounded resigned. "And sorry I am that we canna exist peacefully in the world together, brother."

Brother? Did he mean that literally, or just as a figure of speech?

I rose from the Table's green grass and walked a bit unsteadily to the two men. It was past time for me to join this conversation. I stopped in front of Angus and held out my hand. "You must be Angus MacDubh," I said, proud of my steady tones. "I'm glad to finally meet you. I wasn't sure if you actually existed."

He reached for my hand, but Eoin slapped it away. "I'm sorry, Jane, but I can't allow Angus to touch you."

My eyebrows flew up and my mouth dropped open. "*You* can't allow? What gives you the right to make decisions about who I can and cannot touch?" By the time I finished the second question, my anger had flared, and with it a spark of fire sizzled from my fingertips in Eoin's direction.

I stared at my hand and staggered back, my heart racing.

Eoin cursed and nursed his own fingers.

Angus howled with laughter. "Think ye to control her now that she is a woman grown, Eoin? The more fool you!"

"What just happened?" I cried, no longer concerned with what either man thought. The tangle of my uncontrolled emotions was creating a ball of... something... in my chest. Something that threatened to burst out like the alien from that science fiction movie. I collapsed to the ground, pulling my knees to my chest in a fetal position. Somehow I had to hold it in... whatever *it* was!

"See what you've done?" cried Eoin. "She'll consume herself!"

"What *I've* done," roared Angus. "'Twas ye who made her angry!"

Both men dropped to their knees beside me, but it was Angus who stroked my hair, touched my cheek with gentle fingers, calmed my soul.

And this time Eoin who made no move to stop him.

"Hush now, lass," Angus crooned, his deep voice soothing the raging alien in my chest. "Ye need answers, and we need to give them, but first, ye must be at peace."

Eoin didn't touch me, but he joined Angus in the calming. "Rest, Jane. Let go. Let the power drain away into the good earth of the Quiraing. The Table will absorb the flow, as it has done for our clan for ages long gone."

Under the hypnotic influence of their voices, the *thing* in my chest dissolved, melting away. I could almost feel it seeping out my pores and into the grass that cradled me.

My mind collapsed under the weight of the unknown, and I fainted.

5

$\mathcal{I}$ woke in a stone chamber, bundled in woolen blankets and held securely in a man's strong arms. We sat in a throne-like chair before a roaring fire. The man's linen shirt was soft beneath my cheek and he smelled of heather and lichens. Angus, then. So much for Eoin's decree that my dream man should not touch me.

I stirred, and Angus placed a gentle hand on my head.

"Softly now," he said. "No one will harm ye here."

"I need to sit up," I said quietly. "I need to sit on my own."

"Aye," he said. "I understand."

Carefully, as though unwrapping a priceless piece of china, Angus drew back the blankets and helped me to my feet. My initial impression had been correct, we were in a large stone chamber, like something out of a medieval castle. Angus had been sitting in a large wooden chair, padded with sheepskins and bigger than any modern recliner. The floor was flagged and strewn with rushes. A log table large enough for ten men sat between me and the rough hewn double doors. A second chair, equally as large, sat on the other side of an immense fireplace where red-gold flames leapt and crackled, filling the air with the soft aroma of burning pine.

Eoin sat in the second chair, watching me with brooding eyes. Angus stood, as though to offer me his seat, but Eoin waved him back. With a lazy flick of his fingers and a few muttered words, he created another chair, slightly smaller in scale, from nothing and settled it on the floor facing the fireplace, evenly spaced between Angus' chair and his own.

He bowed his head to me. "If you would join us, Lady Jane?"

I sat down on the sheepskin-padded chair, wondering if it would support my weight or disappear at my touch. It remained as solid as if it had existed from the beginning of time.

"Who are you people?" I asked. "And where are we now?"

Angus grimaced. "We are in my safehold within the Prison of the Quiraing, and glad I am to have your company." He turned a steely gaze on Eoin. "I've been alone far too long."

"Yes, yes," Eoin said querulously, "you've been hard done-by, and I'm the villain of the piece."

"Aye. Ye are."

"Would one of you please answer the question," I asked, more than a little exasperated. "Who are you people?"

"Why, we are *your* people, Jane," said Angus, as if that explained everything. "I am your match, your destiny, and he..." His voice trailed off. "Well, he..."

"Oh for heaven's sake, Angus," Eoin cried. "You're not explaining anything." He turned to face me. "Angus and I are brothers, twins to be exact. Our natures are opposite. Night," he gestured to Angus, "and day," he thumped his own chest. "We are born of a long-lived race that used to inhabit the Quiraing, but has long since fled this earth. We are born of magic and flame, and are immortal."

"Immortal?" I squeaked.

"More or less," said Eoin. "We can be killed, but it's not easy. Especially since we are also wizards."

"Wizards." This was getting better and better.

"Yes, or did you think you'd just failed to notice that chair you're sitting in?"

"Okay, you two are immortal wizards. What does that have to do with me?"

"You're an immortal wizard, too," Angus explained. "Or you would have been had my brother not interfered."

"Excuse me?"

"What he means is, you were prophesied to be his match. To complete Angus and make his power limitless. I prevented that."

"What?" I cried. "How?"

"He used his arts to bind me to this safehold, to keep me imprisoned in the Quiraing." Angus growled. "Then he..."

"Then I stole your soul from within your mother's womb and flung you into the future. I made sure that when you were born you'd have no memory of Angus, or our people, or the Isle of Skye. I made sure you'd be grounded in the heartland of a country that didn't even exist at the time when you were destined to come into being."

"You did what? How did you dare?" My anxiety returned like the whirlwind Eoin had conjured earlier. Swift and strong and untamable. So this was the reason the Isle of Skye felt so familiar. It was my ancestral home. This was the source of the alien that had felt like it would rip me to shreds earlier. It was the inheritance from my distant ancestors— who wouldn't have been so distant if I'd been born when I was supposed to be— my magical inheritance. A power I hadn't known existed and didn't have a clue how to control.

All because this man had interfered in the balance of my life. My life... and Angus'.

The thought of Angus calmed me, and the thing inside... my

power... calmed as well. I turned to him. "Were we really destined to be together?"

He shrugged. "So the prophecy said. But ye were stolen before birth, so we never met in this world." He came and knelt before my chair, dark eyes searching my face, big hands enfolding mine. "I felt ye the moment ye entered the world, but I couldna come t' ye, bound as I am to this place, and I didna dare to touch the mind o' one so young. So I waited, and I watched, helpless to do aught else."

"But you did come to me," I said. "I've been dreaming of you for years."

"Aye, I did, but not before ye were of age. Then I entered your dreams and made myself known to ye, so that when the time came, ye would know me and come to me... just as ye have."

"Right," said Eoin, his voice breaking the spell like the rasp of a file on metal. "All very romantic. But did he ever tell you in those dreams what he intended to do with you?"

A blush heated my cheeks. "No, but he said we were destined for each other. I assumed..."

"You assumed that he wanted you romantically, as any naïve young girl would. You assumed he would marry you," he sneered, rising to his feet. "Well, you were wrong."

6

I gasped.

Angus roared and lunged toward his brother. "Stay out of this, Eoin. Ye interfered once, and still she came to me. Of her own free will, she came. Ye canna keep her from me this time. She's a woman grown, with a will o' her own. This time the prophecy will be fulfilled."

"What prophecy?" I yelled.

Both men stilled and turned to face me.

"The one that says ye are my destiny, and I am yours," crooned Angus.

"The one that says that you will come to him willingly and sacrifice your life to ensure his ascendency," said Eoin, his voice thick with disgust. "Don't you see, Jane? He'll kill you to attain ultimate power over me."

The room stilled around me. Neither man moved. It was as if time had stopped while I pondered their words. While I tried to wrap my mind around what each was saying. Tried to pry beneath the surface to find the truth.

Not their truth. *My* truth.

Who was I?

What was I?

Angus wanted me, that was evident. But for what purpose? Was he the man of my dreams? The love I'd subconsciously waited for? I hadn't dated much in high school or college. Why should I? I knew my love waited for me in Skye. I just didn't know what that meant.

I hadn't seen any overt magical powers from Angus, but he hadn't denied having them. Had he ensorcelled me from afar? Had he entered my dreams to ensure my cooperation with his scheme, this so-called prophecy? Had I come to Skye of my own free will... or had Angus planted that desire and nurtured it over the years until I had no choice but to come when he called?

And Eoin, what was his game plan? I knew nothing of Eoin except what I'd learned on the trail to the Table, and I had no way of knowing if anything he'd said to me was true.

Of course, the same could be said of Angus.

Angus wanted me to believe we were destined to be lovers... at least, that had always been my understanding.

Eoin wanted me to believe that Angus intended to sacrifice me to gain power over him.

But Eoin had admitted to binding Angus to the Quiraing and flinging my soul through time and space. All to thwart his brother.

And what of me? What did I believe?

I released the spell I hadn't known I'd cast and studied Eoin. He was less familiar to me, not having been in my dreams for years, and yet he'd been kind on our hike, and I'd been attracted to him as we climbed. If he'd displaced me in time and space in the belief that he was saving my life...

"What of you, Eoin?" I asked. "What is it that you want from me?"

He lowered his eyes and spoke to the flagged floor. "I want your freedom, Lady. I want you to make your choices without compulsion, to do as you see fit with the life you have been given."

"The life you stole from her," Angus growled. "She should have come into this world centuries ago, when the world was younger."

"When she would've had less choice," snapped Eoin. "When she would've obeyed simply because you were male and she female."

"Our destiny was prophesied…"

"I don't believe in prophesies," I interrupted, causing both men to stare at me. I had made my decision. I knew what I believed, and it wasn't in the power of prophecy.

"Eoin, why do you continue to hold Angus bound to this place?"

"To ensure your safety, Lady."

I nodded.

"Angus, what will you do if Eoin releases you?"

"I will follow you to the ends of the earth, my love, until I convince you that I am your destiny."

"And what does that mean to you, Angus? Do you intend to marry me and give me children?"

"Well, no, I mean, the prophecy…"

"I see. You have my leave to try to convince me to give you what power I may or may not possess, but let me tell you right now, if that means giving up my life, your efforts will not be rewarded. I repeat, I do not believe in prophecies."

I turned back to my hiking companion. "Eoin, I am no longer a child, and while I have no clue how to use any power I may or may not have, I don't believe Angus is a danger to me. I am no longer a naïve young woman. If I ask it, will you release your binding?"

"I will, my lady." He stepped toward me and extended his hand. I hesitated for a moment and then placed mine in his. Our fingers interlocked as if by their own accord. "If I may, I would ask a boon."

I nodded.

"Will you allow me to mentor you in your magic, Jane?" He stared deep into my eyes and I saw within a soul longing for connection, to belong to someone in this world. "And perhaps, one day, to court you?"

My smile reflected the warm glow his words kindled in my core. "I will."

Angus exploded. "Now wait a minute, the prophecy says…"

Eoin and I laughed, gazing into each other's eyes, and answered in unison. "We don't believe in prophecy!"

COPYRIGHT

ALSO BY DEB LOGAN

Children's Stories and Chapter Books:

Cinnamon Chou Files:

- THE CASE OF THE MISSING INARIAN
- THE CASE OF THE GLITTERING HOARD
- THE CASE OF THE RECREATIONAL THIEF
- THE CASE OF THE VANISHING PUPPY

Prentiss Twins Novels:

- THUNDERBIRD
- COYOTE
- WHITE BUFFALO (A KINDLE VELLA SERIAL!)

"Read-to-Me" Stories:

- CHATTERMASTER
- DEIRDRE'S DRAGON
- THE FOX AND THE FLEAS
- MOM'S HELPER
- READ-TO-ME STORIES (COLLECTION)

Short Stories:

- ANGELIC VOICES
- LILAH'S GHOST

Young Adult Stories and Novels:

Dani Erickson Stories:

- Demon Daze
- School Daze
- Family Daze
- Challenging Daze
- Dangerous Daze
- Dani's Demons (Collection)

Faery Chronicles:

- Faery Unexpected (novel)
- Faery Beautiful (short story)
- Faery Unpredictable (Novelette)
- Lexie's Choice (short story)
- Of Dragons and Centaurs (short story)
- Faery Collectible (Collection)

Faery Serial in Kindle Vella:

- Confessions of a Teenage Tree Sprite

Feyland Tie-Ins:

- Emma: A Feyland Dryad
- On Guard: A Feyland Story

Seer Chronicles:

- Terrors
- To Have...and To Hold
- Selkies in Paradise
- The Journal

- PALADIN SHIELD

Siren Tales:

- SALT WATER
- SIREN SURF

Short Story Collections:

- GHOSTS AND GHOULIES
- MORE GHOSTS AND GHOULIES

Short Fiction:

- AMELIA FOX: SPY IN TRAINING
- BEAUTY OR BUTTERFACE?
- RUSH!
- THAT LAKE HOUSE SUMMER

"WDM Presents" Anthologies:

- 2016: A YEAR OF SHORT FICTION
- 2017: A YEAR OF SHORT FICTION
- TALES OF MYSTERY & MAYHEM

ABOUT DEB LOGAN

Deb Logan specializes in tales for the young – and the young at heart! Author of the popular Faery Chronicles series, Deb loves the unknown, whether it's the lure of space or earthbound mythology. She writes about demon hunters, thunderbirds, and everyday life on a space station for tweens, teens, and anyone who enjoys young adult fiction. Her work has been published in multiple volumes of *Fiction River*, as well as in *2017 Young Explorer's Adventure Guide*, F*eyland Tales*, and other popular anthologies.

Sign up for Deb's newsletter and receive a FREE story!

To learn more, visit Deb at:
debloganwrites.com
Or send her an email at:
debloganwrites@gmail.com

ALSO BY DEBBIE MUMFORD

Sorcha's Children Series:

- SORCHA'S CHILDREN (OMNIBUS EDITION)
- SORCHA'S HEART (NOVELLA)
- DRAGONS' CHOICE (NOVEL)
- DRAGONS' FLIGHT (NOVEL)
- DRAGONS' DESIRE (NOVEL)
- DRAGONS' DESTINY (NOVEL)

Signs of the Prophecy Novels:

- YOUNGEST
- SEEKER
- CHOSEN (COMING SOON!)

Gus and Ghost Short Story Series:

- SEVENTH
- SEVENTH: FIRST FRUITS
- DEATH OF AN ALCHEMIST (Uncollected Anthology)
- SEVENTH: THE SAMHAIN DILEMMA

Kristi Lundrigan Mysteries:

- DELECTABLE MOUNTAIN QUILTING (NOVEL)
- FOOL'S PUZZLE (SHORT STORY)
- WILDFIRE! (SHORT STORY)

Logans of Lastalrig Series:

- Her Highland Laird (Novella)
- Her Highland Yule (Short Story)

Red's Series:

- Red's Magick (Short Story Collection)
- Seeing Red (Short Story)

Supernatural Yellowstone Short Story Series:

- Reality Bites
- The Cat Lady of Yellowstone

Universal Star League Short Story Series:

- The Warbirds of Absaroka
- Awakening the Warrior
- Incident on the Odyssey
- The Queen's Captive
- The Lost Colony
- Voyages Into The Black (Collection)

Witchling Short Story Series:

- Witchling
- The Solitary Sorceress
- To Protect a Princess

Stand Alone Novels:

- Second Sight

Short Story Collections:

- Love in a Flash
- Tales of Bygone Days
- Tales of Love & Magick
- Tales of the Unexpected
- Tales of Tomorrow
- Tales of Disastrous Deeds

Short Fiction:

- A Walk with Georgia
- Adrenaline Junkie
- Astromancer
- Beneath and Beyond
- Deep Dreaming
- Delia's Decision
- Ice Storm
- Incident on the High Line
- Miss Bainbridge's Summer Adventure
- Needle-Green
- New Year
- Opening Her Eyes
- Remembrance
- Silver-Tipped Death
- Sisters in Suffrage
- Skye Dreams
- Spinning
- The Tie That Binds
- The Trail Where We Cried
- The White Dragon and the Red
- To Dream of Flying
- Treasures

- WAKINYAN'S VALLEY

"WDM Presents" Anthologies:

- 2016: A YEAR OF SHORT FICTION
- 2017: A YEAR OF SHORT FICTION
- TALES OF MYSTERY & MAYHEM

ABOUT DEBBIE MUMFORD

Debbie Mumford specializes in speculative fiction (fantasy, paranormal romance, and science fiction) as well as mystery and historical fiction. Author of the popular *Sorcha's Children* series, Debbie loves the unknown, whether it's the lure of space or earthbound mythology. Her work has been published in multiple volumes of *Fiction River*, as well as in *Heart's Kiss Magazine*, *Amazing Monster Tales*, and many other popular anthologies. She writes about dragon-shifters, time-traveling lovers, and detectives—whether amateur or professional.

Join Debbie's special announcement newsletter list and receive a FREE story!

To learn more, visit Debbie at:
debbiemumford.com/
Or send her an email at:
deborah.mumford@gmail.com

facebook.com/DebbieMumfordWrites
amazon.com/author/debbiemumford
bookbub.com/authors/debbie-mumford
twitter.com/deborah_mumford

COPYRIGHT